STORY MAGIC

An Age of Azuria Novella

BETH BALL

Published by Grove Guardian Press

Edited by The Blue Garret

Cover design by 17 Studio Book Design

Ebook ISBN 978-1-952609-12-1

Paperback ISBN 978-1-952609-13-8

Hardback ISBN 978-1-952609-14-5

groveguardianpress.com

To the stories that shape us and to their tellers

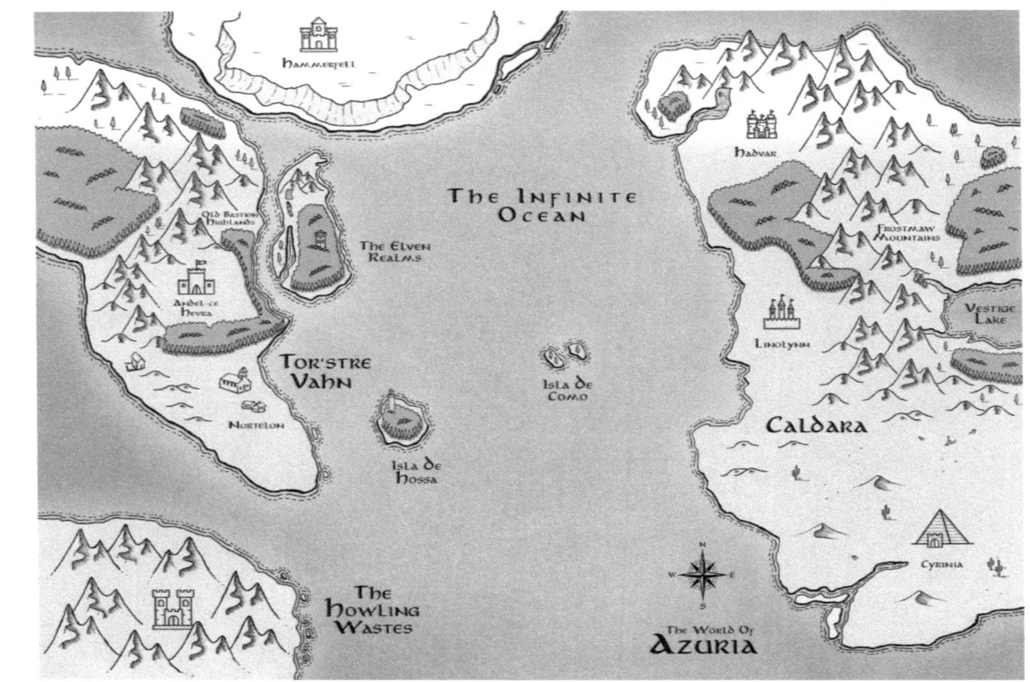

Hammerfell
The Infinite Ocean
Hadvar
Frostmaw Mountains
Old Bastion Highlands
The Elven Realms
Vestige Lake
Linolynn
Andel-ce Hevra
Tor'stre Vahn
Isla de Como
Nortelon
Caldara
Isla de Hossa
The Howling Wastes
Cyrinia
The World Of
Azuria
N
E
S
W

THE GREEN LAW

By order of His Excellence, Senator Antonus Ignatius, with the support and approval of the Council of Andel-ce Hevra and the Priests of Haven, it is hereby decreed that any practice of magic outside that sanctioned and sanctified by the Pantheon Supreme is forbidden across the City of Andel-ce Hevra, the Holy Settlement of Haven, and their Empire.

THE PUNISHMENTS FOR PRACTITIONERS OF SUCH UNHOLY magics are as follows:

For those practicing witchcraft and other magics of the spirit: a life sentence of service and subjugation to the priests of the Holy Settlement of Haven, and the ongoing sanctification that the servitors of the Pantheon Supreme see fit.

For those aiding and abetting witches: following a guilty verdict by the Council of Andel-ce Hevra, life imprisonment and servitude to either Andel-ce Hevra, Haven, or an outpost of their Empire. Alternatively, such persons seeking penance and forgiveness may submit themselves to the mercy of the Council in pursuit of inclusion and initiation into the ranks of the City Watch.

For those practicing the unholy druidic magic of the Vanquished Empress or any magic that seeks to overthrow the power of the Council for that of the earth: execution, the manner and timing of which remains at the discretion of the Council of Andel-ce Hevra and the needs of the City.

For those aiding and abetting enemies of the Empire who revive the unholy magic of the druids and the Vanquished Empress: banishment from the City of Andel-ce Hevra and Holy Settlement of Haven, and a lifetime's servitude to an outpost of their Empire or, given pardon on behalf of the Council, inclusion and initiation into the ranks of the City Watch, as outlined above.

LOYAL CITIZENS OF THE CITY, THE HOLY SETTLEMENT, and outposts across their Empire should immediately report any suspicious magical practice to the City Watch or Council.

The City of Andel-ce Hevra, the Holy Settlement of Haven, and their Empire remain under the protection of and in service to the Pantheon Supreme. We remember the blessings of our gods and honor them and them alone.

CHAPTER 1

"Persephonie, it's time." Felix leaned down from the seat of their wagon to pull her up beside him.

She hesitated, staring after Marcon and Iellieth as they returned to the frenzied activity of the druid camp preparing to flee. The werewolves would be upon them all soon. Gathered at full force, the pack was too large for the saudad or the druids to withstand.

"Persephonie," her older brother called again.

Across the camp, friends embraced, families gathered. They had no way of knowing if they would all survive the fast-approaching onslaught. Persephonie shoved away thoughts of who would remain behind to protect those who fled.

"Felix, we cannot leave them." A rising flood of tears threatened to drown her words. "What if something terrible happens?" Persephonie hugged her arms around her waist.

"We cannot worry about that now." Felix shook his head, his eyebrows knitted together as he searched their muster. "They have a little time to prepare. But Datha is right. This is not our fight any longer. We cannot ask our people to linger."

Their father stood near the front of the line of wagons, muttering with the seers who would guide their path to the Brightlands. It was customary for Datha, as the head of the muster, to consult with the seers about the path across the threads of fate and, together, to select which thread they would travel.

"But—"

Velkan appeared from behind their wagon, his hands seizing her waist. "Up you go." With a gentle push, he placed her within Felix's reach, and her brother pulled her up beside him. For a moment, her former partner's eyes burned as he stared at her. "I'll find Stefan." Velkan nodded to the two of them and strode away to tug their younger brother from whatever curiosity had absorbed him.

"Can we not take Mara with us?" Persephonie leaned to peer past her brother, searching for the druid amid the chaos. Her teacher, her friend—she could not leave Mara to the werewolves. "She could—"

"Persephonie, no." Felix set his jaw. "You know that Mara will not consent to leave her conclave behind."

"But what if . . ." She could not bring herself to say the words. *What if Mara fell to the werewolves and she never saw her again?*

Her grandmother's voice drifted back to her from when they had buried Papu a few years earlier. "What does Fortune's wheel tell us, child?"

Her tear-filled eyes had transformed Babu into a wrinkly blur with black-and-silver hair. She sniffled. "That Cassandra spins our fates forward, and no single event—

good or ill—is a finality. She . . . she assures us that, one day, we will find our loved ones again. Perhaps in this life, perhaps the next."

Babu had squeezed her hand. "He was so proud of you, little Sephie. Your Papu will find you again."

Her teacher would too.

Seeing her stricken face, Felix scooted across the seat and wrapped his arm around her. "It will be alright," he whispered. "It will. Datha will see to it."

She nodded into her brother's shoulder as Velkan and Stefan came back around the side of the wagon. Datha's approach prevented Stefan's questions about why she was upset.

"Are we all loaded and ready?" Datha looked at Felix. This was only the second time her older brother had been fully in charge of packing their wagon and preparing for travel.

Felix nodded. "Yes, Datha."

"Very good." Datha's eyes flitted over to Persephonie, his brow furrowed in concern. "Hop in, Stefan. Velkan, you too."

At the boss's direction, they both climbed in through the half-door behind Persephonie.

Datha walked around the horses and came to stand by her side. "You understand, *cher'a*, why we have to leave?" Her father placed a hand on her knee. "You know that we would stay if we had any other option?"

"I do, Datha. I just wish . . ." She lowered her head.

Her father caught her chin under his finger, drawing her eyes up to meet his. "So do I, Sephie. So do I."

"Boss Cassian," one of the drivers called back from the wagon ahead, "we are ready."

Datha raised his hand in farewell to the druid conclave.

On the opposite side of the clearing, one of the elders raised their hand in return. "Pick me up in a moment, eh?" He grinned at Felix and returned to the head of the muster.

Their father stood with his arms crossed as the seers stepped forward into the twilight, murmuring their prayers to Cassandra. Felix clicked his tongue to the horses, and they pulled the wagon after those in front.

After the first few rows of trees, the forest shimmered and shifted. Shadows grew. The inky outlines of pine, oak, and yew faded to pure black as the air around them glowed the deep amethyst of Cassandra's eyes. Animals, birds, and wind faded away, replaced by the music of the stars.

A wide onyx path unfurled before the saudad, rippling out in advance of the seers' prayers. The strand of fate wove between the realms, guiding the saudad from the forests of Caldara to the wonders of the Brightlands.

They and they alone, Cassandra's chosen people, could travel in this way.

Across the purple sky, the constellations appeared, winking and guiding the way. To Persephonie's left, Lilith danced away from the grinning tigers who sought to imprison her. The ancient heroine's hair trailed long behind her, erasing her tracks from the hunting tricksters.

High above her head, Llewelyn and Pandora clasped hands for the last time. The moment the two sisters released their grasp, the worlds would be split in two, a process of separation, of parting and division, that would eventually lead to the realms of life, Verdigris's sacrifice, the elemental planes.

Datha paused on the trail through the stars, waiting for his children and wagon to catch up with him. He swung up easily into the seat beside Persephonie. "How about a story, Sephie? To honor the road?"

She squeezed his hand. "Of course, Datha." To their right, the glittering stars showed the first of the naiada emerging from the surface of the sea. Persephonie glanced over her shoulder. Velkan watched her closely, and Stefan smiled. "As Cassandra's chosen people," she began, "we alone possess the ability to travel across the threads of fate. It is our greatest blessing and deepest regret, for the one place we can never go again is our home."

A flash of lilac darted past, adding its glimmer to her tale. Persephonie tossed her fingers into the sky after it, and violet fireflies burst into being around her, settling onto her hair and the shoulders of her family.

The obsidian road continued its winding path through stars and stories. The sky glowed from deepest midnight to pale lavender and back. On either side of their thread, trees grew and shriveled, their seeds becoming forests all around them, the cycles of life, of fate, unspooling over and over again.

Her father's dark brown eyes gleamed as her tale continued. With a second wave of her fingers, Persephonie transformed the sparks into tiny flowers that dotted their hair and clothes. "After Orison's fall, our goddess heard our cries. 'Be not dismayed, my children of fate,' she said. 'To you, I appoint a special destiny. You shall make the stories themselves your home.'

"And so from that day forward, the saudad took up the gift, the mission of their goddess, and they became the bearers of the stories through the ages. These stories are ours to tell, just as the new stories are ours to create. This is an ancient magic bound to our people. And when the stories pass through our lips, the world that once was, our long-lost home, it becomes real, alive, once more."

Persephonie waved her hand slowly past her shoulder and head, lifting the magical sparks in a rippling line, mimicking the surface of the starry sea. She took a deep breath and began to weave the goddess's tale.

CHAPTER 2

"DAUGHTERS OF FATE AND MEMORY"

As Cassandra taught us, in the first days, the branches of the world tree grew close. They had not yet been drawn apart by the turning of the ages and the winds of time. Before Verdigris divided herself into three—separating Brightlands from Shadow, with their meeting place between—Ravenna, the goddess of memory, and her sister Cassandra, the goddess of fate, walked arm-in-arm across the plane of nature.

They passed through dales and over mountains. Cassandra whispered glimpses of the future to the trees. Ravenna embedded memories in the earth.

But bonded as they were, the sisters longed for a place where their powers might unite, where memory and fate could blend as one.

The ocean called them to her shores, below a waterfall. The crystal water, carried by mountain streams, churned against the siren sea. Gulls cried high overhead.

This, the sisters knew, was where their gifts would be wed.

Ravenna gazed upon the waters with her sister by her side. A spark blossomed where their hands touched, and there, they both foresaw what would one day be, the separations wrought by the waters of the world. *In a breath, the forest vanished. Beneath the waters, cities fell.* "This cannot be," Ravenna said. "Is there no way to prevent it?"

Division and her minions—the storyteller must here add— did not yet freely roam across the planes.

Cassandra closed her eyes, her arms extended over the rolling waves. Their energy rippled up toward her fingertips, the tendrils teaching her their liquid heart-song. "Prevent it, we cannot, but an untrodden path yet remains."

The goddess of memory smiled at her sister's intertwined phrase. After all, it was unbecoming for a goddess of fate to speak plainly. To do so gave others the impression their destiny was carved in stone and not waiting on the edge of the breeze, to be chased after and caught for themselves.

"Will you take that first step with me?" Ravenna reached out to clasp her sister's hands, but a spray of water dashed up between them. The goddess of memory whirled around to face the tides. "How dare you interfere!"

The ocean burbled back. It ebbed slowly away, face downturned, ashamed. *We meant only to play.*

"Wait," Ravenna called to the tides. Her sister's eyes sparkled, twin reflections of the water. Even now, the sea played out that which Cassandra had foreseen. The waves danced over one another, spilling and splashing to arrive at her side. "We have seen death and darkness in your future."

The water whispered to itself. The goddess's

pronouncement made no sense to young waters brimming with light and life.

"I have a gift for you," Ravenna said, "to help you find your path."

With a swirl, the waters dove around the goddess of memory. "What will you give us?" they asked. "We have little to offer in return."

"You believe that now." The water somersaulted at her grin. "But that will not forever be true. You will see in time." Ravenna's lips pursed as she reached out for the waves. She parted the water, as it would one day part lands, and sculpted a beautiful feminine form from its depths.

Cassandra stretched out her hand to form the eyes, curved and open wide much like her own. "So you might see the way ahead."

Danuae, goddess of the winds, rippled by, high above. She smiled at her sisters' crafting song and dipped down, her gentle breeze forming a mouth so that the figure might breathe and speak. The lips were full, with wisdom waiting behind them. "So your song might reach those who will listen." Her gift bestowed, Danuae drifted away upon the winds.

The flowing hair, Ravenna swirled to resemble the waves. "Remain true to yourself, no matter the tide."

High above, the sister moons shone down. Their luminescence trickled into the dancing waves and blessed the waters with a light all their own.

The aquarian woman before Ravenna opened her eyes. She blinked and extended her palm. "And what shall I receive from you, kind goddess?" the woman whispered in reply.

"One gift more I have to offer, the gift I freely offer all." Ravenna cupped her hands around the water-nymph's face. The waters stilled, breath held. Ravenna planted a kiss on the wet, cerulean crown. "Remember this, Naiada" —droplets clung to her lips—"your nature changes with the tides. One moment, a storm, the next, gentle waves on the breeze."

Cobalt eyes blinked. The words ebbed, swirled deep.

"I grant you the gift of memory, bottomless and wide. Through it, you shall contain all that you inspire: hearts broken and hearts mended, fortunes made and fortunes lost. By sea, fate will be spoken, by river, fate will be tossed."

Clouds of change thundered on the horizon. The tide trembled in reply.

"Be not frightened of your future." She took Naiada's hand. Her sister held the other. Their energy trickled through the water-nymph. It darted out into the great tides. Others sprang to life along the water's surface, bursting forth with liquid arms and shining eyes. The goddesses chanted together: "Sisters, all, to fall, to rise."

The wind picked up once more. It danced through seaweed tendrils, tossed sunlight through their hair. "All shall look to you"—the thunder boomed—"when they remember no more. But you"—Ravenna raised her voice above the growing squall—"will hold the remembrance here within. Come each new age . . . to rise or fall."

CHAPTER 3

Persephonie found it difficult to tell how much time passed on the thread of fate but, after what felt like several hours, the amethyst sky grew lighter, dashed through with rose and the shades of the sunset. The constellations gleamed, their brightest points motes of emerald, sapphire, or garnet. The travelers were approaching the Brightlands.

Datha led the final chorus of one of the saudad traveling songs, his warm baritone carrying the melody across the muster. With a laugh, he clapped Felix on the shoulder and turned to Persephonie before he swung down from the wagon. "Try to set the worries aside, cher'a. The road we look for is the one that finds us."

She smiled in reply and watched as her datha strode to the front of the line of wagons to consult with the seers as to where they would make camp in the Brightlands.

"I hope they pick the summer court this time," Felix said, his eyes staring off into the brilliant ether.

Stefan leaned forward and poked his older brother.

"You're just hoping that the alseid you met last time is still there." He and Velkan laughed.

"Just because you didn't see her . . ." Felix frowned and looked at Persephonie. "You believe me, right?"

"Of course I do." Her older brother made friends wherever he went and often found himself in a romantic entanglement with one of the young females of their muster or someone he'd met on their travels. A few years before, on their last visit to the Brightlands, Felix had gushed about a beautiful fae he'd met in the forest, an alseid with bright green skin and long hair the shade of fallen pine needles.

Unfortunately for Felix, when he took Velkan and Stefan to meet this breathtaking caretaker of the groves and glades, she was nowhere to be found, and they had teased him about inventing false lovers ever since.

For those whose eyes were used to the civilizations of Azuria, much of the Brightlands appeared unsettled, but this was far from the truth. Small communities covered the surface of the lands and the depths of the waters—daimon, naiada, dryads, satyrs, pixies, countless faeries, the fae—spread across four loosely divided kingdoms, each dedicated to a different season in the wheel of the year. In Persephonie's early adolescence, they had visited the autumn court, a world filled with color, harvests, and celebration. "Not the most reliable sorts when you need something done," Datha had told her, gesturing at the bountiful feast and revelers with his goblet of spiced wine, "but there are few so ready to relish the good of the world and the blessings of Cassandra."

The wilds on the far edges of each kingdom were best avoided, so there was limited mixing between the four realms. The dwellers of the Brightlands told many stories about the great evils that lurked in the ancient fae forests, unchanged since Verdigris had first fashioned the three planes of life thousands of years before.

"We still haven't seen the winter court," Persephonie reminded her brothers and Velkan. "It's said to be the most beautiful of the four."

Stefan's brow furrowed. "Do you think they each say that about themselves?"

"I can assure you, they do," Datha said as he returned, grinning widely. His voice boomed with tremors of excitement. "But perhaps you can decide if the winter court lives up to its reputation, Sephie." He winked. "We'll settle along the outskirts, and, after we've made camp, we can pay a visit to the palace of Queen Mab."

Persephonie's fingertips quivered as she reached out to touch the glittering white bark of a nearby birch tree. The strips of black along its trunk glimmered like obsidian crystals, and the bark shimmered bright with frost. She gasped. It was cool to the touch, but not cold. She pulled her fingers away, their tips coated in blue-white sparkles.

The winter court was even more captivating than described.

It was full night when they arrived, the sky an onyx blanket laden with gleaming stars. High above, the sister-moons shone down, bathing the Brightlands in their ethereal light. Tiny faeries flitted between the white branches, adding their crisp glow to the pale blue and ivory of the winter landscape. Beneath the birches, dark red berries peered out from evergreen bushes, and scarlet flowers spread their petals wide.

Datha came to stand beside her and pulled her close with a strong arm around her shoulders. "I hope you like it, cher'a." He beamed down at her. "When the sun is up, we'll go and speak with the fae."

The little sleep she managed was filled with dark, foreboding dreams. There would be time to think on them later, she decided. First, she would meet the denizens of the winter court.

At times when the saudad traveled, especially to a new location, the settled residents met them with fear and dismay. In moments of danger or strife, some misinterpreted her people's timely warnings as a harbinger of the disaster they sought to avert.

But not so with the fae.

A pair of dryads were already milling about the camp shortly after dawn the next morning when Persephonie emerged from her tent. One's bark-like skin was as white as the birches. She wore a crown of mistletoe and winter roses atop her short, silver hair. Her friend was tall, with ebony skin the texture of the black oak. Two pairs of pale blue antlers rose from the sides of her head, and her long, sweeping hair faded from raven to the same shade of blue frost.

They smiled slowly at Persephonie's approach. "Good morning," she called to them in Queran, the tongue of the forest.

A fluffy gray squirrel appeared on the first woman's shoulder. The creature tilted its head at Persephonie. Three sets of wide eyes watched her curiously.

She paused a few strides away. "I hope we are not

intruding on your forest," Persephonie said. "Our seers believed that this area was unoccupied."

"That is as you say, young saudad," the first dryad replied. Her voice carried the crisp bite of a winter wind.

"Though it is now occupied," the second responded. She spoke softly, the whisper of falling snow.

Persephonie believed that their words meant the saudad were welcome, but she wasn't certain. Around them, the muster began to stir. "Might I offer you some refreshment?" It was customary for the saudad to present their hosts with food and drink.

"Winter's bounty can be hard to find," the second dryad said.

"But for those who seek, she will provide," the first added.

She bit her lip. This time, they presented her with either an assent or a riddle. "Come with me." She waved for them to follow her to Datha's wagon. The pair and their squirrel drifted after her. When they arrived, she made a strong tea for the dryads and her datha and listened as he fell easily into the indirect parlance of the forest-dwellers.

SHORTLY AFTER MIDDAY, PERSEPHONIE WALKED ARM-IN-arm with Stefan along the forest trail toward the gates of the winter court. Intermittent arches, pure white and laced with glittering frost, lined the silver path that twisted through the trees.

Behind them, Felix entertained the two dryads, and Datha and Velkan followed close after. Gleaming gates, pure silver, blocked the way ahead. The forest of birches lined the frost-covered fields on either side.

The fae didn't use the gates to secure their realms. But stepping off the path this deep in the fae forest would send a traveler on a meandering journey from which they might never escape.

"A gift must be given to pass into the queen's court."

Persephonie stopped short as a raspy voice emerged from the tree beside her. She peered around it, and a grinning renard, one of the fox-folk, emerged. He stood a few inches taller than her. Large, red ears poked out from beneath a black silk hat. The renard wore a finely made, dark green coat and twirled a polished wooden cane in his furry hand.

Stefan gasped beside her.

"What sort of gift did you have in mind?" Persephonie smiled sweetly. This was the kind of fae game she liked to play.

"I can be quite flexible where gifts are concerned." The renard raised an auburn eyebrow and winked.

"Ahem."

Persephonie knew without turning that the low-throated warning behind her was Velkan's.

"If the lady is already claimed, there are other arrangements we might make." He smiled wider.

"It is not so much a question of claimed or not." Persephonie shot a look back to Velkan and returned her suspicious gaze to the renard. She wasn't going to let either of them ruin her chance at seeing Queen Mab's castle by competing for affection that she had not consented to give. "But if we land upon an entertaining enough gift, what will you do for us in return?"

Datha's chuckle behind her confirmed that this was the right path to pursue.

The renard spun his hat from his head and bowed. "Well met, intriguing traveler—an exchange would be my pleasure. Surprise me, and a handsome guide through the queen's streets shall be yours."

Velkan groaned in irritation, and Stefan snickered beside her.

"With pleasure, Master Renard. We have traveled from distant lands, longing to lay eyes upon the fair fae court of the winter queen." Her eyes flashed as her fingertips extended. She cast a flurry of snow to fall all around them. The dryads sighed happily. "The queen's realm has inspired a memory of an ancient story, held dear by travelers such as we. A story from the roots of the first age, of how the birch forests originally came to be . . ."

CHAPTER 4

"THE BIRTH OF THE BIRCH TREE"

As Cassandra taught us, at the dawn of the worlds, there was a single tree. She stood in the company of the gods and goddesses, at the right hand of Verdigris, the titan of nature. The tree watched as Fenrir created his first people, the daimon, as the waters gave birth to the beautiful naiada, and as Verdigris created the eldest of the fae.

"It is your turn to create, Tree Mother," Verdigris said. "Whatever is in your heart, let it be."

At the urging of the titan of nature and inspired by the wonders of the goddesses and gods, the Tree Mother blossomed, and her seeds fell. "Look after my daughters as they make their way across the world," she said to Verdigris.

"I shall," the titan promised. "Your children bridge the world of earth and the world of air. For that, they will be honored through the ages."

The trees, spread across the surface of the worlds,

began to branch and grow. They burrowed deeper into the earth, becoming strong, and stretched high into the air, becoming free. And as they grew, they took on quirks and qualities of their own.

Beithe, one of the oldest daughters of the Tree Mother, stretched tall and strong, with silver hair and pale white skin, but her eyes remained her most striking quality. Pure black, with a ring of bright green visible only to those brought into the daughter's embrace.

She traveled far and wide in those early years of the worlds' forests. Each night as she slept, she left a silver hair behind, which, in her absence, as the world warmed, would grow to become a birch tree of its own.

The daughter was lovely, but quiet. Her silver hair captivated her fellow travelers, and Beithe rarely spent her nights alone. "Take this," was all she would say, plucking one silver thread from her hair.

Without fail, each traveler would tie the liquid silver around their finger or through a buttonhole of their coat, their hand covering the delicate bow. But no matter how attentively they cared for the thread, within the week, they would find it had left them. The silver lady's hair was ever prone to wander.

Beithe knew when the hair drifted away to form a tree of its own. With each sacrifice, each piece of her she left to a traveler, a wound appeared, a slash on her skin. When the tree wandered off on its own, the wound healed, leaving a black mark against the glowing white of her skin.

The stories about her and the ones she left behind changed. Her remarkable black eyes appeared across the bark of the new-growth trees, dark onyx slashes said to speak of a broken heart.

There was, however, one exception to the daughter's

journeys. A beautiful song floated down to her from over a hillside, and there she found a young woman, strumming a lute and weaving a tale for the entertainment of the mountainside. Did the girl know that the ancient mountains listened? Somehow—Beithe could tell by the tilt of her head, the twist of her lip—she did.

The tree daughter held still, raising her arms overhead. Her green palms sighed in the sunlight. Her silver skin twinkled in its shadow. She closed her black eyes, letting the song drift and drip through the silver strands of her hair.

Melodies embraced by the wind drifted nearer. Beithe longed to look but kept her eyes shut, prolonging the spell.

"Who are you?" The woman with the lute leaned closer, her face inches from Beithe's own. "It's alright, you can tell me."

Beithe remained still.

"What if I sing to you, then, and tell you a story?" The smirk had returned to the bard's expression, audible in the lilt of her voice. Branches rustled overhead, eager assent granted.

The woman settled her back against Beithe's long legs, rubbing her shoulders against the daughter's smooth bark. Her fingers plucked over the strings, searching out a melody. "A sad song languishes on the air," she whispered, "and it is the one I sing to you."

Her voice picked up a tune that Beithe knew well, though she had never heard its swell outside the woodland of her own mind. The verses danced over hills and valleys, traveled mountainsides, traipsed after ice and under gales. But each time when the chorus returned, the slashes that marked Beithe's skin deepened, spread.

The bard sang of a desperate search, an unending

journey to the ends of the earth. But two lines rooted the tree daughter in place. They held the song to her heart, pressed it across the wide stretch of her limbs, her leaves, her bark:

> *Until the day you found me,*
> *unending, free.*
> *On that day of binding,*
> *forever, to thee.*

The leaves rustled in metallic whispers as the woman rose and pressed her body against that of the tree. She kept the song's cadence as she chanted the final lines of her spell. "Be still for once, in this season with me. We'll plant a forest, and from there, be freed."

Beithe opened her black eyes and gasped. For the first time, a familiar gaze reflected back to her. Brilliant green, with a single ring of purest black.

She stayed not one night, but two, by the musician's side. The woman whispered Beithe's song over the mountains, upon the breeze. Her story drifted out from her, swelling around the trunk of each silver tree, deepening the black marks, rippling up to the canopy of silver and green.

As their second night drew to a close and the tendrils of dawn trickled over the mountainside, Beithe closed her black eyes and lowered her silver head. The wind whispered, "It is time."

Green tears flooded her lover's eyes, but the tree daughter knew the season had come. One by one, the musician plucked the hairs from Beithe's head, releasing them to flutter on the breeze. The wind picked up the tears as well, anchoring a gleaming green bead to the base of each fresh growth, drawing its roots into the ground.

With the final hair loose on the wind, the mountains sighed and called the sun to see. She rose over a chilled earth, where a silver trunk stood bare at her lover's side.

But beneath the earth, the magic continued, the charm humming with life as it ran its course. Rivers of roots grew between the young trees, latching one to another, as the single branches had once spread from a shared source.

The woman wandered the mountainsides, her lute abandoned where she and Beithe had once lain. But then, as the first warm breeze returned to relieve winter's chill, beneath the melody of melting snow, a familiar chorus whispered its charms again, drawing her up and away from the darkness below.

A forest of birch trees had grown from the earth, their sprigs spread from threads borne on the wind. The woman's breath caught in her chest as footsteps brought her closer, closer to the center of the valley she'd known.

> *On that day of binding,*
> *forever to thee . . .*

The trees whispered the words over and over again. They knew not their melody.

A smiling face appeared across the largest of the trees. A silver branch extended a lute. Dark eyes opened over the slashes in the bark, irises black but for their single ring of green.

The woman smiled in turn and settled back against the strong, slim line of Beithe's bark, to teach the little trees to sing.

CHAPTER 5

Persephonie's eyes shone as she lowered her arms at the end of her story. The renard's grin glimmered bright. He bowed his head; with a wave of his auburn paw, the silver gates swung open wide. "May I, fair storyteller?" He extended his elbow to escort her inside.

Velkan sighed heavily behind her.

Persephonie stifled a laugh. "You may."

"Given your readily apparent gifts, I wonder if you might perform your tale once more for the enjoyment of the children gathered outside the queen's court?"

A short while later, Persephonie stood in the center of a sunken courtyard that had been made for storytellers such as she. Renard children whose furry heads reached her mid-thigh gazed with toothy mouths agape, holding tight to the hands of their satyr friends. Behind the children, their parents stood in a semicircle, contented smiles on their faces, and the gleaming expanse of Queen Mab's castle stretched to fill the edges of the pale gray sky.

The palace landscape lent itself to a more dramatic retelling than she had first attempted. Ice-blue flowers covered the hard, frosted earth, and the steam of the children's breath condensed all around them. From it, Persephonie shaped a small birch forest, its delicate branches mirroring the perfectly spun wonders of the ice and birch branches of the winter queen's court.

She bowed her head at the close of her tale, and the fae children patted hands and paws together in applause. The children rushed forward, surrounding her with wide eyes and questions. "How do you make the trees from the grass?" one satyr asked. A short, squat renard tugged at her skirt. "Can the queen's birch trees sing too?"

Beyond the circle of young fae, Datha's face glowed with pride. "Well done, cher'a," he called. He strode over toward a cluster of fae parents, undoubtedly inviting them for more fireside stories and dinner that evening.

Stefan wriggled his way through the children and extracted his sister from their admiration and grasp. "That is one of my favorites, you know."

"Thank you, Stefan." Persephonie leaned into her younger brother's side. Stefan shared her fascination with their people's stories, though he recast many of them into song. "One day, will you teach the entirety of Beithe's melody to me?"

"Let us visit the castle first, and then we shall see."

Velkan and the renard waited in uneasy silence on the far side of the courtyard between two white-barked trees. Behind them, twin rows of saplings darkened from ivory to slate to onyx as they wound their way to the glittering entrance of Queen Mab's castle. A spreading chill caught in Persephonie's throat as she lifted her gaze to the fae forest-palace. Towering white trees made up its base, interspersed by ebony glass walls of night and fractured starlight. Courtyards and terraces, formed from woven silver branches, emerged from the intertwined upper limbs, accessible by spiral staircases lit by floating faery light.

❦

"THIS ONE, YOUR MAJESTY?" JULIET'S ENLARGED renard ears twisted toward the courtyard below as she peered over the silver terrace of the fae queen's receiving room. Surrounded by enraptured fae children, a saudad storyteller conjured frosty trees from the mist.

Her tail swished, catching crisp air as she turned to face the queen. To journey beyond the misty sanctuary of Apollo's domain, Juliet and her vulpine sisters had to take physical form. In the fae realms, they favored the figures of the renard, an embodiment of their own foxlike spirit. For this trip, her fur was the color of smoke, and her silky apparel bore the tales of the constellations. "Why would she leave her family and people?" Despite their affinity—or curse—for travel, most saudad remained with their musters throughout the entirety of their lives.

Queen Mab's silver eyes flared. "Why indeed, Juliet Evenstar? Tell me this: Of all the vulpine in Apollo's court, why is it he sent you to my side?"

Answers sparked to life in Juliet's mind as she slowly returned to stand before the braided branches of the white throne. *Because I'm not afraid of you. Because the others resist interaction with the world outside, not understanding that it makes them strong. Because—*

The queen smirked, and Juliet's list fizzled out. "Then perhaps you understand the storyteller in my courtyard better than you first believed." Queen Mab waved silver fingers through the air, dismissing Juliet and her questions.

A flock of feathered fae approached the white throne from behind her to beg for the sovereign's favor and blessings.

"Psst." A green ash dryad beckoned Juliet closer.

Juliet bowed to the queen and scurried across the marble floor to the dryad's side.

"Meet me on the eastern terrace," the dryad whispered.

The music of her voice calmed Juliet's racing heartbeat, and she nearly missed the fae's exit in a whirl of shimmering branches.

Juliet exhaled, inviting calm into her spirit before finding her new acquaintance. She tugged at the shoulder of her gown, yanking it back into place. They had no need of such frippery in Apollo's court, clad as they were in their ethereal forms. But here, among the fae, their essence had to take physical shape. She bunched the gown beneath her fists and slid through the crowd assembled around the queen's audience chamber. Her furry tail swished behind her, the one aspect of the renard form she enjoyed.

CHAPTER 6

Persephonie awoke in a cold sweat. Once again she'd dreamt about her mother being trapped in a market, surrounded by fire, with no way to get out.

She pressed her fingertips to her temples. Dreams had many meanings and interpretations, but each night, this one felt more and more real.

Persephonie pulled her blanket up to her chest and reached over for the deck of cards with the gray-green backs, her favorite for dreams and times of trouble. "When faced with darkness," the elderly saudad woman who had made the deck said, "instead of shutting your eyes, blow out your torch. Then, the stars will allow you to see clearly the world around you."

A single card slipped from the stack and landed on the violet quilt spread out before her. DEATH.

She jolted back away from it.

Without looking at the card again, Persephonie tugged a shawl from her bag and crawled out of her tent.

Datha's snores rippled out of the wagon next to her, accentuated by Stefan's soft breathing. On her other side, a trail of dark footprints had broken the covering of dew leading from Velkan and Felix's tent. Velkan, most likely. Felix was not one to rise with the dawn.

Persephonie tugged the shawl tighter and slipped into her boots. The glittering white of the birch forest waited for her. Perhaps the trees held the answers she sought.

As she walked, Persephonie murmured prayers to Cassandra, beseeching her goddess's help in discerning the best path forward.

She settled at the base of one of the larger birches, the bark a crisp bite against her back. These could be the offspring of that first birch forest she'd spoken of a few days before. Persephonie sighed and hugged her arms around her waist. Staring at the forest, she recalled one of Mara's favorite musings: "The trick to finding answers from the trees is being willing to wait."

Surrounded by darkness and birches, by the glittering blue glow of frost without the cold, wet melt, she readied herself to be patient.

Cautiously, Persephonie pulled at the edges of her dream, drawing it back toward herself. There had been three silhouettes moving near Mama, picking their way through the flames. One was thin with long, flowing hair; another broad-shouldered and strong; and the third, a head and shoulders taller even than Datha, with great, swooping wings.

A shape stirred among the trunks in front of her. Persephonie sprang away, preparing to run, but stopped as a familiar voice called to her.

"Velkan, you scared me." She placed her hand on her heart and leaned back against the tree, trying to slow her breathing.

His dark eyes turned to the ground. "Forgive me,

Persephonie. I was out walking, and then I saw you. I did not mean to venture so close as to disturb you." At her invitation, Velkan sat beside her and rested against the birch's trunk. "You are lost in deep thoughts this morning?"

"I am." The glittering silver branches spread in intricate, intersecting patterns overhead. Before coming to the winter court, she might have thought a sky that changed from black to muted gray and back again would have been depressing. But as the sun rose and cast her glittering rays across the vast birch forest, the earth glowed a pale blue in the dawn light.

The winter forest gave her new eyes for her morning's reading. Death did not necessarily spell an end. Sometimes, it meant a new beginning.

Velkan leaned closer beside her and pressed his shoulder against hers. "Is there any chance you will share them with me?"

Persephonie smiled. "Soon, but not yet."

She would speak with Datha first. The muster did not need her at present. They would spend several more weeks here at least before traveling on. He could spare her for a visit with Mama, long enough for Persephonie to find her in Andel-ce Hevra and ensure that she was alright.

CHAPTER 7

"THE DRAGON AND THE SIREN QUEEN"

As Cassandra taught us, there was once a powerful green dragon who dwelled on an island in the middle of the sea. There he lived, and there he ruled, until he met the siren queen.

After she acquired all the riches and power the sea could offer her, the siren set her sights on land, on the hoard of the dragon king. This dragon did not amass riches of gold or gems, but power through a store of magic. It was said that the dragon's power was so great, he could turn the wheels of time and fate.

The siren bid the waves to announce her coming. They crashed against the dragon's island, and a storm swelled in the offshore deep. The queen spread wide her webbed, sapphire hands, and her shimmering fins sent her up, up, up to the surface of the sea.

She stilled the waves and calmed the sea. For what came next, she would need the salty breeze. The staccato crash of wave upon rock rolled across her emerald tongue.

"Lord of land and lord of air," the siren called the dragon forth, to meet her where the land kissed the sea. The haunting lullaby of distant dreams rose with the tide of her voice, drawing sleepless hearts closer, closer, to better hear the queen of the sea. She dropped her song to the barest whisper, a caress of breath against the ear. "I request an audience with thee."

The siren's call thrummed across the island. Her power, the unanswered question of her song, provoked the curiosity of the king. It's not every day that a siren queen appears, even to a powerful dragon, and he was intrigued. The dragon stepped out of his lair and transformed himself from a great hulking beast to the form of a man with smatterings of green scales across his olive skin and a head of thick black hair. He strode over sun-warmed rocks and approached the siren who waited, half-submerged, beyond the shoreline. Sea-swept hair clung to the siren's scaly form. Her bare body glimmered, sunlight caught at the crest of a wave. Her gray eyes tugged him closer, inviting him to sail upon a storm-tossed sea. "What is it you would ask of me, siren queen?"

For a moment, the siren faltered. She had never laid eyes on one so striking, save perhaps herself, across land, air, or sea. "I wish to share in your power, to change the weave of fate," she answered. "For this, what would you ask of me?"

The sea harmonized her every word, luring the dragon toward the queen. He calmed the echoing melody of his own heart, the inexorable tug of land toward the sea. "The magical spell of your voice will not work on me," he said, and the queen's eyes widened in surprise. Were he bound to land alone, her call would have awakened a desperate longing, a sleeping dragon of its own. But the sea and the air have a more intimate understanding, pressed together in a dance over wind and waves. "Would you offer me riches? Renown? I have all this and more." The dragon stepped nearer and reached out his hand for hers. "Offer me something I do not yet possess, and what you desire shall be yours."

The siren's eyes narrowed. "As you wish, mighty king." She bowed her head, and the tide returned with her to the sea. "I will think upon your offer and return within the year."

She arced over the water and dove beneath the waves, her form rippling like salt upon the breeze. The dragon's breath caught in his throat as he watched her swim away. He smiled to himself. *Such a long time, my siren queen.*

The queen thought long and hard. She consulted the wisest in her court beneath the sea. "We know not the treasure of which the dragon speaks, dearest queen."

She adapted her form, fashioning legs from her fins, so that she might travel the realms of land beyond the sea. The queen consulted with scholars and elves, but they had not the answers she had journeyed to seek. "Visit the ancient fae," they suggested. "Those of Brightlands and Shadow, they have lived long enough to solve the dragon's riddle."

The four Brightlands queens gathered for the first time in an age. "We can answer the dragon's riddle," Queen Mab said with a grin. Wintery frost glittered behind her dark eyes. "But I fear such an offering will not please you, fellow queen." The fae's gaze turned from her sister-rulers to the siren. "Would you grant him your gifts over the sea? The music of your voice that bends mortal knees?"

"No," the siren queen sighed, "these powers I would not concede." She clutched her webbing-less fingers into fists and thanked her four hosts. The siren put the magic-kissed lands behind her. "There is one final realm I've yet to see."

She journeyed through the first of the worlds' trees, through deep-set roots and into the Shadowlands. The siren shivered. How long had she been away from the sea?

The queen walked the dark plane, visiting vast forests and castle grounds that stretched as far as eyes could see. She spoke with rulers and hermits. The siren sang away the horrors that lurched across this land, dark and deep.

I cannot grant the dragon what he has asked of me, she thought. *Yes, doing so would change fate's weave, but that is not the alteration I wish to see.*

"And what is it you wish?" A low voice rose from the shadows around her. The dark coalesced, and a cloaked mage appeared before the queen. He chuckled low in his throat. Bone-white fingers extended toward her. "There are two trinkets you might offer this dragon that he does not currently possess," the mage said. "But what will you give me in exchange for my aid?"

A night and a day passed as they set their terms, and finally, they reached an accord: In three days' time, the siren queen would speak with the dragon, and the prince of shadow would arrive to claim his reward.

The dragon grinned as the siren queen returned to his lair. He had watched with anxious heart as each season turned across the year. *Surely one so clever will perceive how to turn the wheel of fate*, he thought. *Love alone possesses power so dear.*

His smile faltered as he took in the siren's altered form. The sapphire glow of her glorious scales had faded. Shadows clung to the hollows beneath her eyes, her lips, her collarbone. He could not speak above a whisper.

"You are here to make me my answer, are you not, my queen?"

"I am," she sang, her melody ringing across minor tones, "though you may think me a fool that I did not see it sooner."

His heart fluttered, his hidden wings unfurling on the breeze. "We are all prone to foolishness when the right prize crosses before us," the dragon answered. "Come, speak to me of what I seek."

"I give you my heart," the siren queen said to the dragon.

How fervently he had wished to hear those words one year before. He raised a scaled eyebrow. "The heart of a siren queen is not easily possessed," the dragon answered in return.

"Do you accept that which you do not yet possess?" Her eyes sparkled with the light of the sea.

The shadow prince had told her, "Love and betrayal are the key. Offer him your heart, a gift thrilling to any lucky enough to win your regard, but deception is the true gift, and one the dragon has yet to receive. Three nights from now, I will meet you on his island upon the sea. There, I will strip the dragon of his power and grant it to you. In return, you will serve me—and your own whims—till such a time as I see fit. Serve me faithfully, my dear, and in the mortal realms, your power will be rivaled by none save mine alone. I have no desire to limit you, siren queen."

The power of the dragon was more bountiful than the siren queen had bargained for. She had seen his great hoard, but his wisdom of spirit, his abundance of magic, was the prize she longed to possess. With them, fate's wheel was hers to command.

The dragon's eyes softened at the bewitching figure

before him. "If only you had reached this conclusion on your own, beautiful siren, I would have granted you riches beyond your wildest dreams. But you have been won by power alone, and in this, you have spelled your doom. I will not unweave that which you have set upon the loom, avaricious queen. Indirectly, the shadow prince who waits to subdue me will do the same to you. Wait and see."

The shadow prince appeared before them and cast his spell on the dragon great and green. The amber eyes of the dragon bore into those of the siren queen, and his magic wove itself around her, intertwined so long as she lived upon land or sea.

As the ritual neared its end, the dragon fell to his knees before the dark mage and the siren queen. He groaned, "Remember what I have said, my queen. Power is not always what it seems."

The prince of darkness grimaced as his spell was nearly complete. Despite the intricate ties he devised, the edges of the dragon's soul slipped further and further away. He glared down at the dragon on bended knees. "What is this magic by which you resist my binding?"

With a chuckle, the dragon shook his head. "There is much you do not know." His spirit burst forth from the body he had wrought to woo the siren queen. A great winged beast emerged instead, covered over in scales of bright copper and green. The dragon's spirit flew off and away, hidden beneath his island where the queen and the mage could never find it.

All power has its limitations, as the siren soon discovered. She collapsed into the arms of the shadow prince, and he carried her from the island shore. For her treachery, she cannot bear to walk the hallowed ground where the dragon laced a spell of his own. With nearness to the sacred soil, the hole in her heart grows too vast, the result of her pledge to the dragon king.

Still he dwells there out of sight, where his spirit found its home. There he offers rest, respite, for all who wander, desperate or alone. But the dragon's favorite travelers, as the saudad know well, are those who ask, but do not yet know, the path of their own fate. "There are questions we all must ask," he says to the travelers he shelters inside his home, offering wisdom where he can. But late at night, he asks his own: "Will lost loves return to us? Do second chances await upon fate's loom?"

The siren's legend instructs us all to be careful what we leave behind. But still she holds the dragon's heart, as fate and love decreed. Across the lands blessed by the dragon's magic await the same promise he made the queen—Seek out the true desire of your heart and there find destiny at its deepest weave.

CHAPTER 8

The vulpine spirits whispered to Apollo. A long-absent ally approached. Many times he had wondered how long it would be before Yvayne returned to cast her shadow upon his doorstep. Behind his mask, he pursed his lips at her approach. Ravenna's daughter had inherited all of her mother's self-assurance, though Yvayne carried the burden of her experiences with her always. Her mother had cast the weight off.

For dramatic effect, Apollo allowed his wings to swish across the smooth stone floor as he approached where she stood waiting. "The one who travels through mist has come to see me at last." He clasped his hands behind his back.

Yvayne stared up at him, her gaze already challenging his own despite how deep she had descended into his domain. The greatest concentration of his power lay here. Most so mighty as Yvayne avoided spaces that made their opponent more powerful than they would be in a neutral environment, one where the very air could not be turned against them. But Yvayne did enjoy breaking expectations.

Her voice was crisp and cold when she spoke, exactly as he remembered. "Certainly you know why I am here."

With a twirl of his fingers, the entryway vanished behind her. No sense in keeping such a reassuring passage visibly present during her visit. From the edges of the circular chamber, the vulpine spirits whispered. He, too, had been unprepared for her return. "I had expected you to come sooner," he lied. *Tell me why you have come now, Yvayne.*

"I have many pressing matters to attend to in Azuria. You are well aware of this." She continued to scowl, growing impatient already at their reunion.

Apollo set his jaw, willing the ancient spirits to murmur Yvayne's thoughts into his ears.

They emerged like whispers underwater, more impressions than words themselves. She worried about what he would ask in return . . . but in return for what, he was not yet sure.

"I hear your thoughts while you are in my realm, Yvayne." Less a lie than a stretch of the truth, but she was too ensnared inside her swirling concerns to perceive it. "You fear what I will ask of you."

"Your requests have been unreasonable in the past."

The vulpine hissed their displeasure, and Apollo flung his fist up at his shoulder. *Silence.* Did the other guardians have to deal with such undisciplined displays in their own domains? "Mistress Yvayne comes to us for aid," he growled to the vulpine and closed the distance between himself and the fae. He reached out and took her chin between his fingers, a show of strength to counter the apparent laxity his spirit-servants had displayed. "And we are here to help, are we not?"

Yvayne struggled against his hold, her pale purple eyes

blazing into the darkness. She would find a way to make him pay for such insolence. It was perhaps the trait of hers he most treasured.

Apollo feigned a chuckle and released his grip. Had something terrible transpired that drove her, desperate, for his help? He bit his lip behind his mask. If he had behaved differently a few thousand years ago, would he have been the first she called upon, and not a last resort? He changed the tack of his questions, interrupting his own whirling thoughts. "How is your new pet? The garnet-haired druid? Is she indeed one who has returned?" He, too, had been interested in the signs surrounding the half-elf Iellieth, a reincarnation of Rowan, the one whom Yvayne had loved. Iellieth's coming indicated other possible repetitions in the fate-weave that he had long awaited. If Cassandra would grant him a second chance, a new Circe of sorts . . .

Yvayne glared back at him. He should have been more cautious in his reference to her past. Though he had warned her of the dangers of attaching her heart, she had been unable to resist Rowan's charm. "We shall see," Yvayne growled.

She omitted further details on purpose, he knew. Her focus remained on convincing him to intervene. So she was still unaware of his own willingness to act. An intriguing development.

"Lucien's spirit has been sent back to this realm." Yvayne withdrew the ace from behind her back, tossing it onto the table before him. Apollo stifled the rage that simmered to life inside his chest at the mention of the traitorous guardian. "At the very least," she said, "I need to know when he leaves."

"And at the very most, dear Yvayne?" Apollo adopted

the sycophantic tone she despised. He struggled to slow his breath. Lucien, who had betrayed him and his brethren, siding with Alessandra when their own forces were at their weakest.

Yvayne raised an eyebrow. She must have seen through his ruse.

Apollo straightened beneath the fire of her gaze. His wings rippled in response, trembling beneath the shackles of his own reins. *Ask me to kill him, to end his manipulations here and now.* He had most of the pieces in place. What harm would come from an advance play of his own game?

"You could actually exert yourself and try to stop him," she answered simply.

The vulpine howled with delight, anxious to avenge their lord, to extinguish the insult of Lucien once and for all.

But no, not yet. They needed a little while longer. Apollo shook his head, his teeth bared as he imagined Lucien's demise. "What an intriguing idea." He forced a chill of calm across his speech. "But I think not. I won't be swayed so easily this time around." His emotions had gotten the better of him before Eldura's fall, when he played as a puppet directly into Lucien's schemes.

"Do you find this a change from your actions before?" Yvayne's glare darkened as she crossed her arms.

How greatly did she despise him? His every action must appear to her as either selfish or cowardly. But so long as she did not suspect the plans he had already in place—the overflowing rage of the Untamed, perfectly poised to oust Lucien from his deep-rooted position in Andel-ce Hevra— the betrayer guardian and his spies couldn't know either.

Like a leaping flame, Yvayne's thoughts turned to the

Brightlands fae, a fickle alliance to which he himself had already turned. But when she considered beseeching the angels, with their false moral clarity, he could resist no more. "No need to bring them into it." Apollo glowered.

"Name your price, and I'll be on my way."

His price he well knew, but she would never agree. "I'm surprised you think so little of me, Yvayne." He stalled a moment longer and began to pace a circle around her position in the center of the room. Perhaps he could reveal part of his hand so as to better conceal the rest. "You see, I have already begun to play."

"Play?" The spirits roared into his ears, transmuting the rush of her furious thoughts.

Apollo forced himself to laugh. *Retain the appearance of control.* "One of your flock is of great interest to me," he said slowly. Cassandra had sown visions of her for what felt like centuries, the one named Persephonie. "A certain saudad with hazel eyes."

Yvayne's reaction was more measured than he had expected it to be. A rush of purple flames flew at him. With a sharp exhale, he tossed it to the side. The fire sizzled into the shadows below. The vulpine would extinguish its remains, allowing him to focus on the task at hand.

Her thoughts sharpened against him as a blade. *After your failures before*, her whispers joined the ravings of his own mind, *your interference with the saudad is forbidden.* Cassandra would never allow him near her chosen people again.

Apollo clenched his hands tight. "She is only half saudad," he muttered, a consolation he had often repeated to himself when he wondered at the depths of the goddess's cruelty. Surely she would not twist his fate thus without cause.

Yvayne's anger lunged at him. This *saudad* was dear to her as well. "Persephonie is no concern of yours."

He couldn't help himself. Flailing, desperate, he clutched the fae's shoulder. *Please*, he nearly begged. *Give me another chance. I will not fail again.* He steeled himself, hiding once more behind his layered masks. "You forget with whom you are dealing," he whispered as much to her as to himself. "I wish her no harm. Why are you so quick to assume we must all follow Lucien's cursed path?" *I would never hurt her. Can you not tell me you know that?* Apollo unfurled his wings, blocking her way.

Against her will, Yvayne's thoughts answered him. She knew he would not pursue Lucien's twisted fate.

Apollo reined in his surprise and drummed his fingers together to hide his relief. "I have my own promises to keep, Mistress Yvayne." His head drooped with a sigh. Promises to which he would remain true, no matter the cost to himself. Yvayne pulled against him, ready to leave, but he had a final wish to express. "Allow me to offer the girl a measure of protection." *Trust me in this one small thing.*

Yvayne's frown deepened. "Protection? So that you can do what?"

Carefully, he would reveal this aspect of his oath to Cassandra, to serve the goddess of fortune and those woven into the weave of her workings. "I might please Cassandra, to begin with." He paused to study her response. "And I think you'll agree it would be nice to have the fates on our side."

Yvayne's lips pursed. She knew he was hiding something.

The guardian lifted a finger of his gloved hand, adding

a second revelation to the first. "But if that's not enough for you, I have an active interest in the fate of the city." He propped his head onto his glove. Had she truly not suspected his involvement with the Untamed? "The outlaws specifically."

Yvayne slid away from him, her own power restored enough to break free of his. "You cannot be serious."

Apollo smiled. It was a more involved maneuver than he was usually known for. Good. If he could surprise Yvayne, who closely watched all, he might stand a chance at surprising Lucien as well.

"Why?" Yvayne continued to worry about Persephonie, not fully grasping his plans for the Untamed.

A final bit of theater, and she could go peaceably on her way. "I made a promise to help the band of outlaws in the city for my own reasons that are . . . mostly benevolent." It was simply a matter of whose side one was on. "What do they call themselves?" he added, falsely distancing himself from them. "The Untamed?"

Yvayne stomped closer. "Help them how?"

He shrugged and resumed his pacing. "I promised survival, what else?" *Revenge.*

"Survival is not enough," Yvayne countered. With a flash, her fingers extended, and violet flames erupted around the two of them, locking them together in a ring of fire. Her aggravated questioning resumed. "Are you going to actively help them against the entrenched powers of the city? The Council of Andel-ce Hevra is influential enough to send a werewolf pack to destroy an entire druid conclave. Do they have any idea of Lucien's involvement, of his twisted forces strengthening the Council's foul roots? What they're truly up against?"

I am going to help them destroy Lucien, whether they realize the depths of his influence or not. But he couldn't say that, not yet. "No, *they* do not. But I do." He ran his fingers along one of Yvayne's dark blue braids, rousing her anger and distracting her from the game laid out on the table before them. Could she guess the cards remaining in his hand?

A vision flashed across the fae's thoughts, a picture of himself, seen from behind, fists and wings outstretched at the edge of a mountaintop, a city blazing in cruel scarlet light that stretched across the lands beyond. The fall of Respite, the last free city of Eldura.

"That's not good enough, and you know it," Yvayne snapped. "Your followers in the city think of you as a guiding spirit. Someone to help them." She glared as her basest opinions of him returned. "And here you are, playing tricks."

Apollo's jaw tightened. Did it seem that way to Cassandra too? A cheap trick and not a carefully arranged plan?

Yvayne crossed her arms, her deeper suspicions taking hold. "Why are you intervening, then? And tell me, exactly, what your intentions are for Persephonie and how you're going to help her in the city."

That is too much, Yvayne. I will not reveal every layer, not yet. "Or what?" He lingered over each syllable, affected calm dripping from the words.

Her binding fire leapt higher, the purple descending into black. Yvayne's rage spread to the distant stone columns. The vulpine screamed in fright.

Enough. "I've no desire to allow Lucien free rein in Andel-ce Hevra," Apollo explained. "He deserves a challenge at the very least. Which, I surmise by your presence here, you are not prepared to pose, or, shall we say, not yet."

The flames abated but did not extinguish. "And what of Persephonie?"

Ah, the final piece of his plan. He had wondered if she might guess it. "I'll send a vulpine to protect her," he offered. Juliet should return from her scouting in the Brightlands at any moment.

Yvayne considered his offer. "And . . ."

Apollo's jaw twitched. Would he ever be able to regain her trust? "And I'll make sure that she and her mother do more than survive." An easy enough promise to keep.

"Hmm." Yvayne scrunched her lips to the side. She remained unaware of how much Rowan had treasured this precise expression, the powerful fae weighing her options.

Yvayne's thoughts flickered over to Rowan, a possible effect of the ancient spirits embedded in his domain. Apollo's chest seized at the pain reverberating out from her. He allowed her the few moments' retreat, lost in the world of her memories, him by her side as she buried the one she loved.

She needed less time than he had bargained for. "You're not to speak to Persephonie," Yvayne warned.

He nodded. Easy enough to obey for now.

"Or to appear to her in dreams."

Good guess, Yvayne. "As you wish."

"And tell whichever vulpine you're sending that she'll have her hands full."

Apollo laughed. On this, they agreed. Juliet was the only one he trusted with such a task, but the vulpine had proved herself more than capable on delicate missions in the past. "Of that, I have no doubt." Before he could think better of it, he caught Yvayne's hand and gave it a reassuring squeeze. "Thank you," he said softly. It was the beginning of a second chance.

"There's one other thing."

Apollo's breath caught. Had he mis-stepped already?

"If there comes a time when she needs to leave the city or be returned to her people," Yvayne said, "you'll take her if I cannot."

His wings exploded out behind him, and it took all his might to draw them in again. *For that, I am ready at a moment's notice.*

"Lucien has returned to his full strength," Yvayne warned. A scowl crossed her face as she flipped through a list of grim possibilities. They still didn't know what to expect from Lucien, even after all this time. "The girl could be a target if he grows desperate enough. If you won't stand up to him, or at the very least watch his movements, I'll have little choice in the matter. And that leaves her and the others vulnerable."

Apollo crossed his arms. He would protect Persephonie. "I can sense him, but—"

"No." Panic flared behind Yvayne's eyes. "This is not a game, Apollo. We do not know that this opportunity will present itself again."

Her alarm cracked his calm façade. "I'll keep a sharp eye."

"See that you do." The doubting whispers returned, reminding him of the stakes should they fail a second time. There would not be a third. "I will be watching you as you watch her." A quick smile flickered to life across her face. "Perhaps she'll pull you in deeper as I cannot."

Much deeper than you yet know.

"And in the meantime, I have more allies in mind." Yvayne carved an exit for herself in the flaming circle and pranced off toward the hidden entrance through which she'd come.

"Which ones?" Apollo asked warily. *Not the angels, not this time.*

Her eyes flashed as she glanced back at him. "Who do you think?"

He threw his hands into the air in mock irritation buoyed by relief. "The Brightlands fae? You cannot be serious!" Yvayne had such high hopes for them despite their blindness to the growing dark of their own domain. Would she ever extend the same to him? "They're not going to intervene." Apollo shook his head.

Yvayne smiled as she fired her final, knowing shot. "You did."

He sighed as she stepped through the portal, returning to the sunny worlds beyond his realm. "Any word, yet, from Juliet?" he called out to his spirit-servants.

The vulpine crawled back out of the shadows. No, she had not yet returned from the winter court.

Apollo nodded to them. Aside from the mistake at the beginning, Yvayne's visit had been well played by all. "Come and fetch me as soon as she returns," he ordered. There was much work still to be done.

⬥

JULIET'S SPECTRAL FORM SHIVERED AS SHE SLIPPED forward from the crowd of her sisters to hover before Apollo's feet. She drew upon the reserves of her courage, her curious sisters shimmering behind her. Their lord did not like to be questioned, but the vulpine had decided— they needed to know. And, in her absence, they had appointed Juliet as the one to ask.

She stilled her trembling heartbeat and raised her awareness to the guardian's gaze. "Why this girl, Persephonie, my lord?" Juliet paused, calling upon the depths of her being again. "What makes her so special to you?"

Apollo settled back into the gleaming height of his obsidian throne. "You must doubt fiercely to question me so, Evenstar."

"No." Juliet clenched her swirling center tighter. *My sisters do.* He thought she was jealous, or responding with emotion alone like a newborn vulpine, all spirit and passion without sense. "I will do as you bid, my lord. I simply wish to understand." Their speculations had grown more wild as Apollo's fascination grew. But just as it fell to her to see his will enacted beyond the sanctuary of his domain, it was her duty to step forward now, to speak.

Apollo traced the line of his jaw as he considered her question. She and her sisters waited in silence. When the guardian spoke, his voice boomed out across the stone room. "Few of you are old enough to remember the world of Eldura that came before, though its signs and secrets return to us again."

His long, black-gloved fingers gripped the arms of his throne as he leaned forward. "There was a woman who walked the earth in its early days, born shortly after the fall of Orison." The guardian's eyes drifted away into the past, and the winds inside the chamber changed. Scents long forgotten trailed in on the new breeze. "Circe was the first Chosen of Cassandra, though she was not to be the last." Apollo's brow contracted. "The way she moved about the world, even as a small child . . . it was clear to each of us that she would change the weave of fate."

One of Juliet's sisters spoke into the stretched stillness that followed. "And did she?"

Emotions somersaulted in the guardian's golden gaze. Slowly, he ran his tongue over his front teeth. Apollo loosened his hold on the arms of his throne and brought his hand forward, condensing the smoke that cloaked his inner chamber.

The vulpine gasped as the chained silhouette of a male figure appeared out of the fog. He slumped forward on his knees, arms bound and stretched to the side. Juliet's heart leapt into her throat. Hanging above the man on the back of his cage was a broad set of fae wings. Aside from those that graced the back of Yvayne, she had never seen their equal.

"Can you answer their question, Emryc?" Cold fury swirled in Apollo's eyes.

Emryc, the fallen immortal who had failed the guardian on his sacred quest many millennia ago.

The bound man raised his eyes to their master's. Hatred flared across his face, crystallizing in his forest-green gaze. "Not to your satisfaction, Apollo."

Juliet's sisters hissed at the prisoner's address of their lord. Few had earned the right to avoid the guardian's honorifics inside his own domain.

Apollo bristled, but his anger did not yet break. "I gave you a very simple mission, Emryc." Daggers clashed in the guardian's voice. "Protect her, and bring her to me when her mission to Cassandra was complete." His lips tightened into a thin line, and he snarled. "Because of *you*, Circe is dead."

"She is free." Each word thrummed as Emryc spoke, a drumbeat and a reprimand.

Apollo roared, his rage shaking invisible iron bars. He stomped off the stone dais and towered over Emryc's chained form before turning his back on the prisoner. The guardian faced Juliet and her sisters. "The goddess Cassandra does not idly extend her favor. Those who would serve her and the workings of fate find patterns that indicate the rare position of Cassandra's chosen. Circe bore these signs, millennia ago. They dance now over Persephonie Arelle."

Apollo spun to find Juliet among the crowd of spirit-servants. The gold in his eyes illuminated the chamber surrounding her, and her sisters backed away. "You, Juliet, will serve as her protector." His jaw ground back and forth.

Juliet dared not interrupt until he had finished speaking.

"Emryc, this will be the last chance for you and your cursed line." Apollo's voice had dropped to a whisper.

The bound man raised his head, stillness settling over his body as the guardian dictated his fate.

"Your final heir will guide Persephonie as she serves Cassandra," Apollo continued. "Your heir will bring her to me when her task is done, her people saved." The guardian swished his cloak to the side as he strode across the chamber floor. "Doing so will restore your wings to you and cast a new hope over your descendants." The sharpened edge returned to Apollo's voice. He settled back onto his throne. Emryc and the vulpine had yet to move. "Fail me again, and you will lose much more than your wings, immortal one."

Apollo smirked as his words struck the captive. "You may go." With a wave of Apollo's hand, Emryc's cage once again disappeared. The guardian glanced at Juliet and pointed to the spot before his throne.

She approached, and her spirit knelt before him.

"I know you will not fail me, Juliet Evenstar," her lord said. Apollo drummed his fingers together as he mulled over the tangled threads of fate. "I will place Emryc's heir outside the city in a position to aid both you and her." The corner of the guardian's lips turned up. "Persephonie knows a version of Circe and Emryc's tale, though it is more, shall we say . . . romantic than what truly transpired." Apollo glared over her spirit at the swirling shadows where the caged figure had been. "We must play the hand Cassandra has dealt with control and calm." He lowered his voice as though they were the only two present in the room. "Do not reveal to Persephonie who or what you are. The time for that will come but is not yet nigh." The guardian bowed his head to Juliet, dismissing her.

Juliet drifted away from her lord's audience chamber. She glanced back. None of her sisters were watching. Juliet steeled herself and dashed off to Emryc's holding cell below.

❧

"I'VE NO DESIRE TO SPEAK WITH A SPIRIT-SERVANT." Emryc turned his face away from Juliet, avoiding her as best he could despite the gripping binds of his chains.

"Have we not similar goals, you and I?" Juliet slid closer to the side of his cage and slipped back into her renard form. Perhaps a physical body might make him more comfortable.

Emryc growled in reply.

Juliet settled onto the cold stone floor. If necessary, she could wait out the fallen fae.

The prisoner's shoulders tensed. Finally, he lifted his face and glared at her. Belief fueled by hatred burned in his dark green eyes. "If your goals dictate that you do as your lord bids, then no, we remain at odds."

She scooted closer so that her furry toes touched the

outer edges of his iron cage. "But why is that? I wish to understand."

Emryc studied her closely. She sensed he would never fully trust her or one of her kind. "Know you the story of my curse, vulpine servant?"

In her heart, Juliet rebelled at the reminder of her rank in Apollo's court. Did not the guardian explain himself to her and her sisters? Had he not appointed her to a special task? She wouldn't let Apollo's prisoner raise her fur. "I do not, Emryc."

"How is it that I find even that small insult a surprise after all this time?" Emryc grumbled, more to himself than her. "No one ever reveals that the most damning part of a curse is that both it and you may be forgotten." He dropped his gaze, and a shadowy weight descended upon his shoulders where wings had once been. "I failed to return Circe to Apollo's side when her quest for Cassandra was done." Emryc's voice softened, drifting out of his cage toward Juliet on the fickle winds of memory. "She begged me not to," he whispered, "and I couldn't find it in myself to refuse her."

A single tear plinked onto the slate stone before him. "Breaking my promise to Apollo was the purest penance I could manage, but it was still not enough to atone for my initial betrayal, for her not knowing how I found her, or at whose behest." Emryc shook his head. "The loss of my wings, the curse of immortality, and the extinguishing of my line are small prices to pay." His breathing slowed, and his evergreen eyes returned their stare to Juliet. "With everything that I am, my one hope is that my final heir has the strength that I found only at the end."

Juliet frowned and leaned closer. Her wet nose sat

parallel with the iron bars. "The strength to do what? I do not follow your meaning."

The prisoner sighed. "The strength to tell Circe what serving at her side meant to me." Emryc shook his head, his gaze drifting into the past once more. "I should have confessed the truth of my heart to her every day. That was my ultimate failure, beyond any of the rest. And so every day, from now until forever, I find myself alone, bereft of the companionship I held and hold dearest in the world." Emryc settled back onto his heels and laid his chained hands on the floor of his cage.

The prisoner went on to explain how Apollo had loved Circe too, as had several others. But that didn't matter to Emryc so much as the words he had neglected to say, a nuance Juliet still could not internalize. She and her sisters knew one another's thoughts. They communicated without words. Were not the actions of physical beings the same as their shared emotions?

"I came to Apollo in a time of desperation," Emryc said with a wry smile, displeased, she thought, with himself. "He granted me might and immortality in exchange for a single favor, the protection and escort of a vibrant saudad in whose future he had a vested interest." Emryc explained how his resolve had cracked as the time to fulfill his bargain to Apollo drew near. He knew Circe would be devastated at her binding to the guardian, another apprehension Juliet struggled to understand.

Emryc refused to tell her how Circe had died, only that he ensured her spirit would pass on to Astralei. The saudad would not even risk her soul returning to her people to be born anew at a later time. "I did as she wished," was all Emryc said. His mocking half-smile returned. "I doubt that I need to tell you of Apollo's anger in the matter."

The open scars down his back where the roots of his wings had been said enough to Juliet. She shuddered at the pain her lord would have been sure to inflict.

"I will tell you one final secret, Juliet Evenstar." A sudden calm cast a shadow over his face. "Apollo will never forgive me for what I did, though he has no notion of his own hand in Circe's fate." A spark of rebellion flashed behind green eyes. "Before and after you meet Persephonie, you would do well to consider your own choices, the magic you give, and the surrenders you make in serving the guardian's will above your own wisdom." Emryc strained against his chains to peer over his shoulder at the outstretched wings on display behind him. "Wings are but a small price to pay."

CHAPTER 9

"THE FIRST CHOSEN OF CASSANDRA"

As Cassandra taught us, dark are the tales of the vast Underland, the interlocking caverns and caves where few mortals dare go.

But Circe, the only child of the famed saudad Boss Miren, was no ordinary mortal.

The saudad traveled deep underground on a quest from Cassandra herself, to end a war that had burbled up from the depths some forty years before.

The goddess of fate had marked Circe as her chosen representative upon the planes of life, casting rainbow strands through her long onyx hair. An iridescent shimmer clung to the saudad's skin, another token of favor from Cassandra.

Fortune had seen fit that a winged warrior join Circe on her quest—Emryc, a fae from the Shadowlands, sworn to serve the saudad and her goddess. Their journey underground together was to be their last.

Circe had already proven herself to her goddess and

her people when dreams from Cassandra bade her to brave the Underland. A powerful fomorian general, Daugath, had seized a thread from the weave of fate. Cassandra couldn't have such potent magic falling into the wrong hands. "Take care not to fall under their spell, my chosen," the goddess warned. The lords of the Underland had long been known for their cunning and beauty. It was by these traits that they turned away from the gods themselves. In the earliest days, this ancient race of fae took powers only the gods had known into their own hands. And ever since, the destiny they sought to forge was entirely their own.

Out of this independence, scorn grew, rooted deep. The fomorians despised those who honored the gods in the lands above. They were quick to charm surface-dwellers away from their sun-kissed homes, most eager for those blessed with magic, a power they sought over all else.

Circe's emerald eyes danced as she accepted the quest from her goddess. A plan was already taking form before her. Her unique magical prowess would make her the perfect temptation for a fomorian general. From there, she and Emryc would set their trap. "Thank you, Cassandra. I will not fail you."

For three days, Circe and Emryc journeyed deep into the earth. As she kept watch on the third night, a shimmering amethyst gem appeared from out of the swirling black before her. Circe smirked at the jewel. "Who are you, and why have you come?" She softened the trebles of her voice so as not to wake her companion.

A deep-throated chuckle echoed all around her. "You know who I am, Chosen of Cassandra. But I can allow you and your companion to go no farther."

The whites of Circe's eyes flashed in the darkness. "And why, Daugath, is that up to you?"

Their banter filled the bleak spaces of the caves. The fomorian tried to entrap the saudad in complex riddles while she wove delicate story threads that would form the tapestry through which to cast her own charm.

Hours later, Emryc jerked awake beside her, wrapping his hand around the hilt of his greatsword. "What is that?" His wings stiffened as he glared at the floating jewel. "My lady, have you had any rest this night?"

"No." Her half-smile soothed his reproof. "I have done something much better instead."

The gemstone floated nearer. In a whisper of movement, Emryc placed himself between Circe and the stone.

But the saudad shook her head. "Daugath does not represent the danger we had feared." She squeezed Emryc's forearm, hoping to calm his suspicions. "There's been a change in plans." Daugath had convinced her, in their wide-ranging talks through the night, to aid him as he used the thread, altering the weave to their collective best advantage.

Lavender light flared around the gemstone. It rippled over the darkness of the caves, flowing outward to embody Daugath in ethereal form. His figure towered a head taller than Emryc. Behind his spectral shape, the severed strand from the weave of fate, a piece as long as Circe's arms and thick as her wrist, pulsed with Cassandra's amethyst glow.

Daugath inclined his head to their wide-open eyes. "As I reveal myself to you, I reveal also a problem and a plan." He turned to Emryc, recounting what he had explained to Circe in the night. "The leader of my people, King Lefre, has grown careless and cruel," Daugath said. "His endless wars and campaigns against Lightdwellers must come to an end, lest he lead the remainder of our people to ruin." Daugath had studied the thread of fate, internalizing its intricacies. Many tiny threads, some representing an entire life, others a moment, made up the strand Daugath had seized at his king's order. "With this," he continued, "we shall garrote his leadership when he least suspects our arrival."

King Lefre, Daugath told them, had mounted many attacks against those who lived in the lands touched by sun. He had ordered his agents to collect the most powerful and beautiful from the settlements they struck and to drag them into the dim depths of his domain.

Daugath's hope for a peaceful future bewitched Circe as he spoke. Surely it was for this vision of a new era that Cassandra sent them into the vast Underland. Not three weeks before, the king's forces had butchered an entire saudad muster. Try as they might, they could find no trace of the few he had captured. The rest, his merciless soldiers left to rot in the sun. Circe was determined to protect her people from such assaults again.

"We will attack in two phases," the saudad continued with her eyes aglow. She turned to Emryc. "I do not think you will like our plan, but you must trust me."

Emryc's gaze darkened. He had heard similar warnings from her before. Each led to her putting herself in unnecessary danger.

Daugath's gemstone guided the travelers through the winding routes of the caves, the amethyst drifting before them and lending its light. The general showed them the safest passage up the river and warned them of the many-legged dwellers of the Underland's intricate caverns.

"Wait there," he said as they neared a large opening.

A heavy form shifted behind the nearest cave wall. Footsteps caused tremors in the earth.

Shing. Emryc whisked his blade from his back and positioned himself in front of Circe.

Cassandra's Chosen waited quietly. Her lips curled as the magical amethyst drifted forward. A towering figure emerged from the cave, and Circe's breath stuttered in her throat. The gemstone returned to its rightful place in the fomorian's chest. Circe met Daugath's eyes for the first time. The scent of damp, underground mosses swirled through her nose, the deep-set roots of an ancient oak mingling with firesmoke on a rainy citrus breeze. She stumbled a half-step forward and laid a hand on Emryc's broad back, steadying herself. Daugath's physical form possessed a gravity all its own. He emanated a sense of destiny, a heart's call, the likes of which she had only felt once before.

The general stared down at the two of them as he stepped outside the entrance of his cave. Like his spectral form, he could have fit Emryc beneath his chin, and Circe barely came to the center of his torso. Shadows shifted across his dark skin, and the amethyst heightened the purple tones of the swirling mist.

She stood eye-to-eye with the shimmering gem. "General," Circe purred, sweeping into a low curtsy.

He bowed in return. Daugath's icy blue gaze pierced the darkness and cast a white light over their upturned faces. "Allow me to welcome you into my abode."

Daugath spread before them an elaborate sketch of the fomorians' settlement, an extensive system of caverns and chambers carved, over millennia, from the rock of the earth.

Emryc studied the parchment while Circe observed

the general's makeshift room. A few notches in the walls served as shelves while others held glowing lavender stones, paler than the one the general wore embedded in his chest.

Her fingers glided over one intricately carved stone. "What are these?"

"Don't touch that!" Daugath snapped.

Circe yanked her hand back.

White light blazed in the fomorian's gaze.

"I am sorry," Circe whispered. "I meant no offense."

Daugath lowered his head and slowed his rapid breaths. "It is I who should apologize." He sighed. The gem in his chest pulsed, a thudding heartbeat. "They are the souls of my companions. I must return them to the halls of our ancestors." The fomorian ran his tongue over sharp, canine teeth. "Our fool of a king wasted their life-energy in his endless quest for power. But by their sacrifice, I will put an end to his bloated, foolish reign."

The fomorian general explained how he and his companions had overpowered the general assigned to retrieve the thread of fate from the saudad muster. Circe steeled herself, holding tight to Emryc's hand as Daugath described the slaughter they had inflicted. "I could not risk sparing them," he said with eyes lowered. "Lefre's thirst for power is too great. He will keep attempting to destroy your people for your influence over the weave of fate." Daugath had convinced several fellow soldiers to turn against the general on their mission and seize the thread for themselves. They had fallen in the fighting that ensued, Daugath the only one of their number who survived.

Though he had taken the thread from the general's possession, Daugath had been unable to prevent several of the other soldiers from returning to the king. "This puts us at a severe disadvantage," Daugath said, "one I hope the thread can help us to reverse. I have studied it for the last several days," he continued. "With your help, we can manipulate its influence to remove Lefre from his position of power."

"And who will rule in his stead?" Circe's mind still reeled from Daugath's tale of violence against her people, suffering she herself had witnessed. How long would Lefre keep the survivors alive?

Emryc understood the fomorian's expression before she did. "Ah," he said, shaking his head. "You will, of course." The winged fae's scowl had not lessened since they first encountered Daugath in the flesh. "How do you know that we can trust him, Circe?"

She didn't have a definitive answer for him, only her intuition. "Cassandra sent us on this mission, not someone else. There has to be a reason for that. Something we could see or sense that others might not."

❦

THEIR PLAN UNFOLDED TWO DAYS LATER.

Circe took a final glance over her shoulder at Emryc as she followed Daugath deeper into the caves. According to the general, her understanding of the king's proclivities was correct—King Lefre would find her to be an incredibly tempting offering, one Daugath would make to ease the sovereign's suspicions and win back his place at court.

"It's just the magic," she added to Emryc before he could object again. With his bevy of raids over the years, Lefre had developed an extensive, loyal army and had little need of warriors like the winged fae, even one with his extensive skills. But magic, the essence of the divine weave that held together the fabric of their worlds, was always advantageous. And, as Circe had learned long ago, the more magic one had access to, the more powerful and promising its wielder's fate might be.

"It is a relief to hear only your thoughts and not his," Daugath said as their first hour alone in the caves came to a close.

"Hear his thoughts?" She was unsure what he meant.

The fomorian chuckled. "Are you not supposed to be a wizened storyteller, Chosen of Cassandra?"

Circe crossed her arms in mock irritation. "*Supposed* to be? I am. A storyteller, that is."

"Then you know the stories of my people and our abilities," Daugath intoned, no longer posing the idea as a question.

She had heard stories about the fomorians' special traits before their separation from the gods. Their magic was unique among the worlds' earliest peoples. It centered around abilities of the mind, such as the perception of another's thought. Many storytellers had speculated that it was due to these powers that they had decided to part ways with the divine order. As legend held, the fomorians had sensed something in the gods' plans, or their very natures, that made separation, darkness, and condemnation more promising alternatives than obeisance in any form.

Circe carefully considered her response before she answered. "I have heard many stories of your people, enough to understand that half-truths and exaggerations dwell among the rest."

The fomorian paused, glancing back at her.

"Shades of stories indicate truth, not falsehood," she

clarified, a smirk playing at the corner of her lip. "It is when a single story stands upon the field, alone, that we must be most on our guard."

Daugath turned back and resumed walking, his scowl showing the way before them.

If she could find a different way of explaining her meaning to him, the intriguing, storied nature of his people, perhaps he might trust her more, view her as a desired ally instead of only a necessary one.

"Statements fall like feathers from a bird," her mother had taught, the muster's children gathered in a knot before her. "But stories are the birds themselves." Boss Miren had lowered her voice, inviting the children closer into the glow of her wisdom. "A single feather can tell from whose back it fell," she had said, "but only the bird herself can sing."

Circe's heart squeezed tight inside her chest. She could feel once more the heat from the pyre where her mother's body had been burned after her death, setting free her soul upon the wind. One of the seers had stood by her side, shedding silent tears as the flames licked across her mother's shroud. When only ashes remained, she clutched Circe's elbow and whispered, "When you enact the teachings of those who have passed, they live on in you." The seer had bowed her head and drifted away from the flames, leaving Circe alone with her mother's lingering spirit.

Circe brushed aside a tear. The seer had envisioned this moment, among a handful of others, and had wanted the boss's daughter to be prepared. Perhaps a story of her own might help Daugath to see. "Before this journey," Circe said, "after a great loss, I experienced a period of doubt. Not in Cassandra's plans or abilities," she clarified, "but in my own." Circe rubbed her chilled hands over her arms. She hadn't shared her misgivings with anyone. How was it that Daugath, this near-fabled creature she had only met a few days before, could be so much easier to talk to than Emryc at times? Perhaps she was being unfair. She could discuss many things with her fae companion, but her misgivings about her own potentiality . . . he was not willing to hear. And when she most needed his advice, he was always quick to assure her of the security of their shared fate.

Me being the "Chosen of Cassandra" means nothing to Daugath. My goddess is just as lost to them as a life lived without the sun's rays. To Emryc, the significance of her title seemed clear. *But I am still myself*, she wanted to say. *Only Cassandra's overt recognition of me has changed.* Was Daugath listening to this jumble of thoughts, the tangled trajectory of her own misgivings? She stole a glance up at the fomorian. His face, this time, remained blank.

"Cassandra sensed my apprehension," Circe explained, "and she answered me simply. 'Life *does* transpire as the stories tell,' she said. 'Remember this, and you will always find the right path ahead.'"

"And you find this muddled pseudowisdom to be help-ful?" Daugath scowled down at her, the pale blue ice of his eyes bright against the pressing dark of the caves.

Circe grinned. The goddess of fate would have found it amusing too. Doubt wasn't frightening to Cassandra. She simply waited for it to disperse and allowed the wheel of fate to turn itself. "When the time is right, it will be."

Daugath shook his head, offended at the lack of logic involved in Circe's path-making. "I respect your people's valuation of stories, but how are you to know which story you are in if that is your gauge of measuring the correct-ness of your path?"

The saudad laid her hand on her heart. "We sense it." Circe patted her chest. "Here."

The fomorian groaned and turned away, striding past her to take the lead through the tunnels. "That cannot be the case. You would already be dead." His disbelief and amusement brightened their surroundings and buoyed Circe along. Being alone in her beliefs was easier, lighter, than others—even those she loved—affixing their faith to her. If she and Emryc failed, Daugath would move on to the next logical step in his plan. Her own actions, however brilliant or misguided, couldn't shatter anything he held dear.

☙❧

CIRCE STILLED HER SENSE OF RELIEF AS DAUGATH brought Emryc to the foot of King Lefre's throne. Each step had transpired according to plan thus far. The king had accepted the gift of her and her magic with glee, and Daugath had excused himself to fetch a second gift. She couldn't risk betraying the fear she had felt at their separation or the fact that she knew the man being brought before the fomorian king.

Her hips swayed as she swept forward with the line of servants. Whatever their position in his house, Lefre clad all in his service in sheer, flowing fabrics—the sensual display meant to enthrall visitors with the influence and pleasure Lefre hoarded.

Daugath's eyes flickered over her before he returned his attention to the king.

As usual, Emryc's expression was rigid. He harnessed his energy and focus whenever they were on a mission, laying bare his years spent fending for himself in the wilds of Eldura.

But as she met his gaze, Emryc's sharp stare clouded. His lips parted as he watched her, singling her out among the many males and females lined up on either side of the king. A soft ripple ran its way down his wings. Had anyone noticed the movement besides her? *He's trying to ensure that I'm alright*, Circe said to herself. *Nothing more.*

The warrior's stiffened shoulders remained squared toward her as he angled his face to the fomorian king. Floating lanterns, coated in colored glass, drifted along the length of the receiving rooms.

"A fine addition to my court," King Lefre's voice boomed in the common tongue. He stretched his broad hands to the side, encompassing the width and breadth of the hall and their surroundings. Where Daugath's skin was purple shadows and slithering mist, the king's figure rippled in muscle and flame. "It is not so fine or useful a gift as the one you first brought, but I accept this addition to forces I trust you will soon be ready to lead."

Daugath bowed low before the king. His displeasure at such a display radiated out from him. So wrapped in his own concerns, could the king not sense it? "You honor me, Your Majesty," the general answered. "My deepest wishes are for the strength and renown of your name."

Emryc inclined his head but kept his eyes pinned on their host.

The king nodded, his red face splitting into a grimace. He waved his hands in Emryc and Daugath's direction. "Make our new addition comfortable," he ordered. A trio of captive courtesans swept forward, looping their bared arms around Emryc's and leading him to the chambers beyond the throne room. The warrior's jaw twinged as they led him away—he had been certain the entire enterprise was an elaborate trap, rigged by Daugath and set up for the fomorians' entertainment.

"I swore an oath to Cassandra," he had said to Circe before they parted. Conviction burned behind his evergreen eyes. "I swore to stay by your side and to protect you, just as I have sworn to serve her." His words wrapped piercing thorns around her heart, and she hadn't yet been able to shake the feeling they'd given her. He had sounded . . . hurt, somehow, by her belief in their plan, offended that she might find the risk worth the reward.

Emryc had caught her by the elbow as she and Daugath began to depart. "I know you want to protect your people, but I care not for the fomorian's hopes to free his own from their tyrant or the prospect of peace it might bring." His grip loosened, but he did not let go. "If our fortunes turn, I will abandon all pretenses and get you out of there." Emryc released her and stepped back.

The warrior's stare lingered on her as Daugath led her away into the caves. It perched on the back of her neck as they disappeared from his sight. When a sudden shifting in the dark startled her, she would imagine Emryc swooping toward her, his eagle's wings unfurled, his expression a snarl of rage.

CHAPTER 10

"Cassian?" Yvayne stepped around one of the saudad wagons, searching for the muster boss.

"*Varra.*" The saudad nearest her bowed their heads as she passed. "Varra Yvayne."

A booming laugh rang out from one of the larger wagons, and Cassian emerged at the end of the line, shaking his head. "We will see about your story, Mama," he called back over his shoulder. Yvayne had met his mother on a few occasions over the long years of their acquaintance. There were hardly any as sharp-eyed or with such a gift of Cassandra's sight. "Varra Yvayne!" Cassian cried when he spotted her. "Come, come!" He waved her into an embrace.

Yvayne kept her arms rigid by her side, but she had learned long ago that resisting Cassian's exuberant greetings was futile. Ever since she had aided Persephonie's mother with interpreting her visions, he had insisted that she was part of the family and would be treated as such. He could not be reasoned with in such matters.

The saudad leader frowned down at her. "You are cross, Yvayne? Why?"

"Is Persephonie here?" Her agitation had grown in each moment that passed without the young, boisterous saudad running up to greet her. Perhaps she was off exploring the wonders of the winter court and would soon return.

Cassian's face fell. "No, Varra, she insisted on paying a visit to her mother. My cher'a had troubling visions, and I cannot deny the warnings of Cassandra when they visit us."

Yvayne nodded. She had feared as much. And without Persephonie here, she would struggle to determine whether the visions truly originated from the goddess of fate or if the guardian Apollo had undertaken a manipulation to pull the girl from her family. "Perhaps we might speak?"

The saudad bowed his head and led her over to his wagon. His two sons and another young male lounged behind Cassian's place in the camp. The three rose. "Varra Yvayne." They looked from her to Cassian. She would wait for him to decide to include them in the conversation or not.

"Yvayne, my sons, Felix and Stefan," he said, indicating the tallest of the three with black, tousled hair, and the lankiest, whose straight locks fell to the tops of his shoulders and who held a book in one hand. "And Velkan, who is like a son to me." He was more muscular than the first two, and his hair a dark brown rather than pure night.

"I have come to speak to you about Persephonie."

"What has happened?" Velkan stepped forward, scowling.

Yvayne whirled around at his tone. As though she would allow danger to befall Persephonie without intervening. Velkan bowed his head in apology, and she returned her gaze to Cassian. "Your daughter has caught the eye of one of the guardians," Yvayne said. "Apollo."

A ripple of unease crested over the saudad. "He has aided Cassandra in the past . . ." Cassian frowned. "But why my Sephie, and why now?"

"I could not glean a direct answer from him, though I did force a promise that he would not interfere in her path save in an instance of immediate danger."

"Boss Cassian, you cannot allow this," Velkan interrupted. "What if Apollo tries to take her below? How are we to stop him?" He exhaled heavily as Felix's and Stefan's eyes turned to their father. "Persephonie does not belong in the Shadowlands." Velkan looked from Cassian to her and back. "Please, we have to do something."

"Hmm." The saudad crossed his arms. Cassian knew as well as she the tales of guardians' infatuations through the ages. Apollo would never intend Persephonie harm, but danger followed close behind the protectors of the mortal realms. "I have just returned from traveling with her to Andel-ce Hevra," he said. "She was certain that a looming danger threatened her mother and wanted to warn her." A brief smile flickered across his expression. "Esmeralda and Sephie, they dwell near the pulse of life."

"They do." Yvayne grinned, thinking back to when she had first met Persephonie's mother Esmeralda in the ancient grove outside her home. It had been Esmeralda's sight that had confirmed her suspicions that the wheels of fate were turning once more, Esmeralda who had first seen Iellieth clearly. Yvayne had long suspected that the destinies of Persephonie and Iellieth would be intertwined.

Perhaps Persephonie was currently seeking that same

fate. "I will keep a close eye," she promised. Unlike Apollo's word, hers she knew she would keep.

Should she warn Cassian about Lucien's involvement with the senators and priests of Andel-ce Hevra? She had not yet discovered the object of the mage's manipulations in the ancient city.

"Tell me," her old friend said.

Yvayne sighed. As ever, Cassian was quick to discern the thoughts she preferred to leave unspoken. "Lucien holds the puppet strings of the Council of Andel-ce Hevra. He has set his sights on capturing Iellieth, yes, but that does not mean Persephonie is free from his designs."

"Then we must go after her," Felix interjected. "Datha, we have just begun to see what he is capable of. We cannot leave Persephonie alone to his whims."

Cassian furrowed his brow. Fatherly concern and deep wisdom of the workings of the world fought across his features. They waited in silence for him to decide. "I will speak with the seers and ensure they are watching over her too." He met his son's eyes. "In this way, she is not alone." Cassian placed one hand on Felix's shoulder and one on Yvayne's. "And we must not forget, Sephie walks beneath the eye of Cassandra. Do we trust the goddess to guide her way?"

Persephonie's younger brother, Stefan, was the first to speak. "I trust Persephonie to follow where her heart leads."

The uneasy silence stretched its wings again. Stefan spoke truth. The question, then, was where Persephonie's heart wanted to go.

CHAPTER 11

"Cerdris, have you met our newest taverness, Persephonie?" Otmund smiled in a way that could only indicate self-satisfaction. "I have a feeling you'll get along." Otmund gestured across the tavern to a young female in colorful garb, her every movement marked by the clinking of her many bangles.

"Is that so, Otmund?" Cerdris raised an eyebrow. "And why is that?"

Tess glided by, eavesdropping on their conversation as usual. "Because she's a storyteller." They sighed, casting their eyes up to the dark wood-beam ceiling. "Can't you tell by looking?"

Cerdris hid his grin with his wineglass. "You'd think so at this point, Tess," he said. He drained the goblet and plunked it down onto the tabletop. "You'd think so."

Tess made their round of the tavern's tables. They nodded to two of the other patrons, a man and woman Cerdris recognized but whose names he never remembered. Persephonie stood behind the bartop, polishing the emerald-colored goblets. She stopped as Tess drew close and nodded over their shoulder in his direction.

Persephonie brightened and spun toward him. She gave a soft gasp before abandoning her post in a jangle of glass and jewelry. The tassels from the sash around her waist echoed the flow of her hair as she swished over. "Tess tells me you are a storyteller?" She gripped the edge of the table, her gaze dancing from his face to the parchment and quill laid out beside him.

The new employee of his favorite tavern was even more striking up close, her bright hazel eyes gleaming in the low light, accentuated by the deep auburn tones of her hair.

"Well, I'm fond of writing things down." Cerdris pressed his shoulder blades back into the wood of the booth. He should probably count himself lucky that the figure before him was decidedly feminine or he'd never get any writing done. Collecting the slabs of gossip he found on the city streets and fileting them into pithy morsels for the competing guilds of corner street-criers was difficult enough without added distractions. The ambiance of Otmund's tavern provided him with the space to think, to create, and to dream. Each day as he gazed out of the colorful tavern windows, he renewed his promise to his young, idealistic self—eventually, he would find adventure and romance. He would craft stories truly worth telling.

Her eyebrows contracted. "You do not write down stories?"

And with the accent too, intoxicating. Cerdris flashed what he regarded as a disarming half-smile, though she seemed unfazed. "I like to think of myself as a writer." He shrugged. "Otmund said he thinks we'll get along. So you're a storyteller too?" Not the most eloquent as far as leading questions went, but he'd heard worse before.

"My people and I are made of stories." She pursed her lips and narrowed her eyes. "Though I believe that all people are. We are just more aware of it than most."

This was almost too good to be true. "We being the saudad?" *Please say yes.*

"Yes, of course."

Perfect.

She dipped her head in a mock-bow. "Is my Torstran convincing enough that my accent now goes unnoticed?" The saudad laughed as she slid onto the opposite bench, freeing him from the need to decipher whether she was serious or not.

"Cerdris," he said, extending his hand to hers.

The bangles along her wrist jangled once more. "Persephonie. Charmed."

This was exactly the sort of newcomer Drugas had asked him to seek out. In exchange for his cooperation with the City Watch, he'd received a shortened sentence and a reduced fine. He'd thought Drugas was joking when he first offered. The City Watch was never lenient, especially with those who bore even a passing connection to the Untamed. Cerdris hadn't *intended* to be caught up with the revolutionaries, he had explained after his arrest. It was simply a case of an impassioned romance and unfortunate timing.

Luckily for him, the dashing Captain Drugas had also been quite taken with him. Mutual attraction always helped in these situations. Cerdris could have sworn that the man studied his lips as he laid out the terms. "We want to know who's inside our borders," Drugas had said. "It's a question of safety for us all."

Slipping information about the saudad to the captain would be harmless enough, and it wasn't as though Persephonie was doing anything wrong. Drugas had even promised ten silver coins if he could record something useful such as the future plots of the Untamed or how long they waited to draft new potential citizens into their traitorous nets. Such a reward would free him up to travel to the lands beyond Andel-ce Hevra. He could seek the stories that grew in the wilds, as his own heroes had done.

Cerdris pulled his sheaf of parchment over in front of himself and picked up his lucky quill. *It's fortunate I brought you along today*. The barbs of the raven's feather were still soft against the pad of his thumb. "Can you tell me an example of one of these stories? I'm curious to discover how indeed they 'make us up,' as you say."

The saudad wiggled back and forth, drawing her feet up under herself on the wooden seat. "What sort of story are you in the mood for?"

"Surprise me." He raised his eyebrows with his smile.

Persephonie scrunched her features together, studying him.

"What is it?" Had his eagerness given him away? Otmund would be furious if he found out. He refused to have any dealings with the guards. But really, this wouldn't do any harm.

"I am asking Cassandra which story to tell you first." Her hazel eyes glimmered. "I will start with one I do not think you will have heard."

CHAPTER 12

"LEGEND OF THE BLACK OAK FOREST"

As Cassandra taught us, in the days before the parting of the seas, a great green oak grew.

She stretched high, her canopy rising above all the other trees, and from there, the oak watched and waited.

If anyone had paused to ask, however, the tree would have confessed she was not sure what she was waiting for.

But fate would not hold out forever. There came a day when the tree's fortune turned. And in this changing of her fortune, her fate affected that of so many more.

A young woman came to the oak, desperate for love. "There is a man where I'm from who longs to marry me. I know I'm meant to be with someone else, but I don't know whom."

The great green oak thought this over. It wasn't customary for her to be sought in matters of the heart, though she was keen to try her hand at a subject readily practiced by sages across the land. "Very well, I shall do my best to help you."

The woman smiled and wrapped her arms around the tree. "Thank you," she whispered. "How shall I pay you for your aid to me?"

Laughter rustled the tree's slender leaves. "You need not pay me, child," the oak finally said. "But here, take this." She dropped an acorn into the girl's hands. "This piece of me will travel with you. Plant it where the roots of your heart find their resting place, and I will continue to guide you."

The young woman was overjoyed at this prospect. She tucked the acorn into her pocket, planted a kiss on the bark, and skipped off into the forest.

That afternoon, the young woman returned home to find that she and her family would be going on a trip, leaving behind the suitor she did not wish to wed. "Where are we going?"

Excitement glittered in her mother's eyes. "Do you feel that, child?" she asked, gesturing to the open carriage window once they were on their way.

The girl leaned out, and the wind rushed through her hair, but she could not find the sensation her mother had indicated. "No, Mama, I do not."

The bronze-skinned woman brushed her daughter's hair back away from her face. "You will, my daughter. A change of fate drifts down from the moon and the stars. It calls to you, my child." She smiled. "Be sure to answer, when the time comes."

With a nod, the young woman pressed her palm against the acorn in her pocket. Even from afar, the wisdom of the oak fluttered down to her.

Their carriages drew to a halt once they reached a

verdant kingdom, its borders enclosed by a protective mountain ring. Inside, celebrations stretched as far as the eye could see, from the smallest villages to the grand castle itself, where guests arrived from many distant lands. The time had come, the girl soon came to understand, for the kingdom's lord and ruler to choose a bride. And though she was but one of many, in a twist of fortune that caught many by surprise, the young woman—of relatively minor birth—captured the affection of the lord of the land. Each day, he took her for a turn through his gardens, asking what might best please her eye and make her wish to stay.

The girl returned his attentions with kindness and respect, which made her mother proud. But despite the elegance of the castle, still she missed the simple forests of her home, and she longed for the company of the green oak tree. Her oak possessed a wisdom, a light. When she was with the tree, the girl felt herself swept away into a grand adventure. The *right* suitor, she decided, would bring with him a similar sense.

And then one night, as the girl stood out on her balcony, overlooking the moonlit gardens the lord was reviving for her, a masked suitor climbed the terrace to the girl's rooms. She gasped and backed away as he swung onto the balcony.

He raised his hands, covered by black leather gloves, and asked her to wait before she screamed. "I know I am not alone in seeking your heart," the masked suitor said, "but please, will you give me a chance?"

The masked suitor perched on the balcony's rail, and the girl leaned against the ivy-covered castle wall. He wove stories for her about realms and worlds beyond any she'd yet seen. His tales whisked her away on an oak-scented breeze.

She hurried through each day, anxious for the return of the moon and the moment when she could sneak out onto her balcony. There, she would find the masked suitor, even in the rain.

He made her his offer, the opposite of the lord's. "Come away with me," he would say. "Let me show you these distant lands. We'll adventure together, travel hand-in-hand."

The desire to accept grew and blossomed in the girl's chest. But his stories had brought with them a stronger sense of her tree. Each night as he held out his hand and asked her to leave, she paused, listening for the oak's melody on a distant breeze.

And without fail, her tree answered her. *Wait, not yet*, came the oak's whispered reply.

"Not tonight," the young woman answered.

The masked suitor bowed his head and rose. "Then I shall return to you tomorrow." He planted a kiss on her hand and slipped away.

The lord of the land, at her request, wove a colorful tapestry of fragrant blooms across his gardens. Courtiers journeyed over the mountain passes to visit the enchanting flora, the living testament of love and patience that would win the young woman's heart and convince her to stay.

On midsummer's eve, the lord appeared late at night outside the young woman's door. "Take a starlit stroll with me," he asked. She expected her secret suitor at any moment, but she was in no place to refuse a man of such great power and influence.

The lord led her to the fountain that had been erected in her honor, depicting a shy forest nymph that bore the young woman's face. "Marry me," he said, kneeling down on one knee.

Pain flashed across the young woman's face. "I cannot." She clutched his hand in hers and revealed the secret she had determined to keep. "There is another whom I love, though I do not know his name."

The lord lowered his head, his hands fumbling at something by his side. Watching him, her heart raced. Did the lord mean her harm, here in the beautiful garden he'd made? Or could he accept being second in her heart, the first place shared between the man who told her stories and the wise oak tree?

When he looked up at her once more, a familiar mask covered his face. "My darling," he said, "did you truly not recognize me?"

The woman and the lord married in a ceremony of feasting and light, and the sun smiled down on the kingdom for a year and a day. In the center of the flower garden, the bride planted the oak's acorn, a reminder of her home.

But a shadow fell upon the kingdom in the woman's second year as lady of the land. A blood sickness afflicted her, arising shortly after she conceived her first child.

The lord and the oak did all they could to save her, but the magic of their love was not powerful enough to undo what fate had wrought.

A great storm arose, come to claim the young woman's soul.

Lightning crackled in the sky overhead. The lord cried out as his wife's body fell limp in his arms. "Will no one help her?" His voice lashed across the air. He leaned outside to beg the sapling oak planted below. Her branches quaked in the swelling winds. "Can you not save her?" The lord's voice broke, and he clutched her body to his chest.

The tree's young heart had grown brittle as the sickness took its toll. She could not bear the darkness that had taken hold of her mistress. Another lightning bolt cracked nearby. A branch crashed to the ground, shorn from the trunk of the tree. She screamed in agony. The broken branch gazed up at her, weeping freely beneath the rain.

"The young woman is sunlight to me," the tree screamed at the sky.

Silence glared down, cloaked by the black storm clouds.

The lord's sobs pattered all around her, acidic drops of rain.

Very well, the tree resolved, *then I shall grow of my own accord. I need not your light and will learn to feast on shadow instead.* The oak dug her roots deep, severing her connection to her friends nearby. They cried out in pain and withdrew.

Plunging beneath the fungal forest at her roots, the oak found the darkness she had promised to seek. Tied to the Shadowlands, the oak feasted, her roots wrapped around rocks, breathing the still, clouded air.

Her trunk rippled and waved. Leaves writhed at her fingertips.

Globs of green light splatted onto the ground around her. The tree's wounded neighbors slurped them quickly up. They lifted their roots and crawled further away.

The oak shook as the shadows took hold. Their darkness splintered up her bark. Her branches rasped, water and sunlight no match for the writhing dark that stretched so deep. The leaves along her branches turned black, and she laughed in her despair. "Here, now, fate will see what destruction her negligence has wrought."

The lord's grief erupted once more, thunder ricocheting against the billowing clouds.

"It is time, my lord," the oak cried. "Together, we shall make them rue this day."

As the young woman's spirit seeped forth from her body, the lord and the oak ripped their lands free of the threads of fate, tearing them asunder from the weave of their world. As the woman exhaled her last breath, the grasping dark gripped the edges of the lord's lands and drew them into the umbral realm below.

Back in the girl's homeland, a web of shadows reached the great green oak. They whispered grievous news—the young woman she loved was no more.

The oak's screams echoed up from her roots, floating out in twisted scents upon the breeze. She sagged onto the forest around her, but there was little the smaller trees could do. The saplings growing in the shelter of her shade had not the wisdom to aid the oak in her grief.

"We can help you," the shadows whispered, "only let us inside."

A gap in the center of the tree yawned open, split where the girl's kiss had been planted. "Can you fill what was taken?" the broken oak asked.

"No," the shadows replied. "But we can make the void grow so that you know nothing else."

"Is there no hope, then?" The oak clung to her final moments of freedom from the drowning waves of her loss.

"None that we nor any around you can provide." The wording was so careful, we cannot say the shadows lied.

"Very well, do what you must." The oak bowed her head as she welcomed the shadows inside.

They howled through her depths, claiming each space that was free.

Like her daughter oak, planted in the young woman's

garden far to the north, the tree rained green droplets of light on the forest around her.

"We will all know the loss of the young woman," the smaller trees cried, slurping up the green light that fell around the oak's sides. The verdant beads twisted, tainted, maimed, and mangled.

"And we will remain, and wait, for revenge on fate," the oak said.

Sprawling out from the oak, a black forest took root. At its heart waits her new, twisted form. Gnarled branches and bark stretch toward the sky above, and dark poisoned roots reach into unseen lands below.

As the years passed, the trees' grief grew and spread. The black forest crept up and over mountains, expanding their range. Gradually they advanced, the scent of death their perfume.

CHAPTER 13

"You're certain?" Senator Antonus Ignatius paced back and forth before the oread's cell.

"Yes, my lord," the fae creature wheezed. Her gnarled hands swirled over the milky crystal ball. Inside, a dark-haired figure sheltered close beside Antonus's son. A burbling fountain spit water behind them. "The saudad girl is not alone," the creature explained, unaware of the irony. "Nor is she unprotected. But her spirit spells doom for you and your line."

His true lord had warned Antonus that a female caster might try to interfere. But Lucien had neglected to adequately describe the adaptive calculations through which the traveler would bewitch his son Rennear.

Antonus's jaw clenched. Must these beasts always speak in riddles? "And what of my son?" Rennear remained flighty despite his training and the heightened stakes. Soon, Antonus had promised Lucien, without the senate to coddle the city, and without the false spiritualists to lead them astray, the subjects of Andel-ce Hevra would be brought in line. Rennear, as one of the captains of the guard, would have no choice but to comply. But rid of the saudad's spell, he would see the wisdom of this in time.

"She will divide you further from the one you call your own," the oread said. A grating cough racked the creature's lanky frame. "Her magic is powerful, an antidote to your efforts, though its breadth she does not yet know."

He threw up his hands. His son was a romantic, just like his mother, regardless of the lycanthropy running rampant through his veins. "Very well, seer." He nodded to the two guards who stood watch over the fae. "It may eat today." His eyes flashed over the oread's cage. The fae's bark-like skin had faded, smoothed, during its incarceration. If it lived long enough and served him well, there might come a day when it could pass for human, at least from a distance.

"I expect more precision upon my return." The senator swept his cloak to the side and spun out of the room.

Two more of his guards joined him in the hall, his servant Rigalto sniveling close behind. "Where is my son?" Antonus freed his hands from his gloves one finger at a time. "See that these are cleansed." He pushed the soiled leather into Rigalto's chest. He had not been forced to touch the creature this time, but he would not risk having even a mote of its green magic found on his person. "This too." He swept the cloak from his shoulders and tossed it to the servant.

"Yes, sir." The elderly werewolf bowed.

"He's out riding, my lord," the tallest of the guards replied.

"Well enough." Antonus scowled. He could not reveal the half-truth of this claim without explaining the fae creature and its seeing orb. "Find Eustace for me." Though the werewolf had underperformed at the scene, he might still prove himself worthy of redemption. "A violation of the Green Law has come to my attention. I'd like him to see to it."

"As you wish, sir." The two guards bowed and left his side. Antonus swept down the hall to his office. A senator's work was never finished. They would need to act carefully and outside the council's knowledge, but with a clever plan, an elite group of his werewolves could wipe the saudad from the city streets.

Antonus suppressed a grin as he imagined reporting to Lucien the unrivaled success of their scheme. Turning the saudad girl over to his lord would benefit them both in the end. Lucien could absorb her magic as he had the other druids', and Antonus's son would be freed from her enchantments.

CHAPTER 14

"THE SACRIFICE OF VERDIGRIS"

As Cassandra taught us, the worlds originated in darkness, and from this darkness, a spark of light. Out of the first division, two sisters emerged—Pandora and Llewellyn, separate and together. "You take the light," Pandora said to her shimmering sister, "and I will be infinite."

Llewellyn consented, not then understanding the breadth or implications of the words her sister spoke. Though she kept her later wonderings secret, she did question—what if, from the beginning, they had chosen togetherness and not division?

But such a path was not to be.

The Light divided herself into aspects, separating out fire and nature, water from earth, light from air. The Darkness made fewer concessions. She wove together the bindings of darkness and space, sending her ebbing waves ever further out along the horizons of existence.

As these elements came to be, the sisters' powers deepened. They wove together the worlds, creating the titans and the first deities from the energetic contrast of their opposite natures. As the light grew taller, it grew brighter. Pandora's darkness plunged ever further into the depths.

Llewellyn hid away inside her twisted feelings about her sister's expanding power. She did not name them, and she did not look. The lock clicked into place, and the prime goddess of light turned back to the care and sparks of life that enveloped her days.

The prime goddess of darkness knew better.

Pandora made no secret of her expansive ambitions. She bid her creations to grow in their own power, to spread their influence and their abilities, and to craft new corners of the worlds.

But in Pandora's heart, the love for her sister still survived. Each evening, she remembered their time spent together, just the two, hand in hand, in moments that, at the time, had comprised the entirety of the universe.

It was Pandora's discerning eye that saw the rotting corruption inside her sister, the root of jealousy grown deep. She smirked and called to Llewellyn. Her dark violet hand wrapped around her sister's golden arm, and she pulled her nearer. "Inner darkness grows more powerful away from the light," she said softly. "I made a deliberate choice, those many years ago. The answer to 'why' will always be multiple." Her brows contracted as she squeezed her sister's hand. "You would do well to accept the same."

Llewellyn heard her sister's words, but it was already too late. The shadows inside her had grown long. Their tendrils wrapped around the corners of her eyes. This blindness made her miss the spark of light within Pandora —the sign of unison between the two as they'd had in the first days of the worlds.

Over time, their separation grew, and the division of the first goddesses multiplied across their created realms.

All would have been lost were it not for Izadra and Verdigris.

The titan of nature, Verdigris, perceived the rising smoke between the two powers, the tempers that receded but seemed, nonetheless, only to gather strength for their retreat. She watched as Llewellyn struggled to assimilate the darkness inside herself. The goddess blamed her sister for her corruption. She saw a stain and not unity.

By then, many years had passed since Verdigris had first witnessed a flare of light within darkness, inside the deepest recesses of Izadra, the titan of space. The two fell in love, and in this, they found their way.

They spent hours together on the Plane of Nature, Verdigris's peridot arms wrapped around the nighttime splendor of Izadra's skin. Clear waters trickled by, enlivened by the babbling brook of the two titans' joy in one another. *This*, the air around them seemed to whisper, *this is what togetherness means. This is how the world ought to be.*

The tension between the two prime goddesses grew. They clashed at their meeting places between the planes, their enmity dividing the fae and giving rise to fiends and angels. The titans, perceiving what their creators could not, created the guardians to stand in the balance, to stem the tide of forces raging between the light and the dark.

As tempers rose, it became harder for Verdigris and Izadra to spend time together. Division sparked between the first creations of the prime goddesses, Ilona and Nyx, the titans of light and darkness cast in the picture of themselves. "We must do something," Izadra said. Her gaze burned as she stared into Verdigris's eyes—Izadra and

Nyx alone among the titans knew the breadth of Pandora's power. However noble Llewellyn thought her own cause, it could not withstand the might of the forces of darkness.

Verdigris's own love of darkness allowed her to perceive its snaring thorns in Llewellyn's core. "You are right," the titan of nature said. She pulled Izadra's amethyst lips to hers, savoring the final kiss in their nymph forms. "We will have to show them, my love." She placed her fingers against Izadra's mouth, stemming the tide of her protest. "You and I have learned to reconcile the two." A salty tear carved an emerald path down her cheek. "We will have to do it together. I am not strong enough on my own."

As the forces of the prime goddesses gathered for a battle that would have destroyed the vast stretches of the universe, Izadra took Verdigris into her arms for the last time. She buried her face in her lover's neck, and the two transformed back into their bodies that contained entire worlds.

The vastness of space divided nature into three—three lands, three expressions, separated from one another but held in the close grasp of the black, starry sea.

Izadra's cry pierced the front lines of the gathered forces, driving both sides back and away. Llewellyn called out for Verdigris . . . but she received no answer.

Pandora bowed her head. Slowly, she parted the sea of her servants. She placed a kiss upon Izadra's forehead. And then the prime goddess of darkness walked away.

These divisions are what make our world so beautiful, why nature herself is more complex than we can ever express. The heart of a titan burns inside of her, a titan desperately in love with the intricacies of space—a space that has fully surrounded her in her tight embrace.

What at first seemed like division turned out to be love. In her separation into multiple expressions of herself, Verdigris showed us the way. She saw the brightness and the shadow, and she found the meeting ground between them.

Izadra held her together as she accepted these three separate parts of herself and bound them to one another. The starry planes capture our souls when we pass on, they guide us on our way between Brightlands and Shadow, between the prime plane and her two borders.

Like Verdigris, from whose sacrifice we came to life, each of us are three in nature, we who walk the plane of life. Mind and soul, light and shadow, with our body between, joining the two.

There is always more and always multiple, as the prime goddess Pandora would say. Nurture that which grows within—we are creatures of the Light and the Dark, of Nature and the Stars.

CHAPTER 15

Apollo paced back and forth, his wings trailing the ground. "Where is Juliet?" he growled. He peered through the mists that separated the planes, Persephonie's form a glowing shadow in the center of his domain.

The reflection spell allowed him to perceive what the young saudad could not. Beyond the tavern walls, werewolves approached Persephonie's temporary home, and her vulpine protector was nowhere to be found.

His spirit-servants whined to one another in reply. The vulpine did not know.

Apollo's jaw clenched as Persephonie emerged into the darkness of the street, unaware of the dangers that lurked in the shadows. Was Lucien watching the same scene unfold from his umbral-cloaked lair? The guardian roared, his cry echoing around his domain. Whatever it took, he would not allow her to fall into the lich's clutches. He would keep her safe from Senator Ignatius and his foul master, even if it meant revealing his hand in the ever-recurring game.

He should have encouraged Aylin to attack the werewolves before the apex of the Hunt. But how could he have known that Cassandra would send Persephonie into the heart of the growing conflict? Why had the goddess sent warning visions that would usher her toward danger rather than away?

Apollo shook aside Yvayne's warning at the impracticalities of his attachment. The weave of fate, Cassandra's blessings, glowed all about Persephonie. Yvayne could see it as clearly as he. For those who lived on through the ages, such remarkable magic could not be ignored or resisted. The young saudad would have a special role to play in the events fated to unfurl in the months ahead. Persephonie would need a powerful entity watching over her.

If Juliet didn't appear soon, he would journey to Andelce Hevra himself. Apollo's shoulders seized. By then, it might already be too late.

The guardian tightened his fists. He murmured the spell that would split the planes.

Juliet darted from the shadows and leapt to Persephonie's aid. Apollo expelled the breath from his chest. *Thank the goddess.* His most daring vulpine slashed at the werewolf guards, protecting his charge.

But she did not fight alone.

The shadows at the end of the alley stirred once more. Apollo frowned. The russet-haired guard from the fountain returned to her side. Moonlight clung to the silver of his sword as he slew his brethren, freeing Persephonie from their claws.

Apollo turned away from the look in Persephonie's eyes as she stared up at the mortal man. This pain he had felt before and, so long as they succeeded, he would feel again. That was not the problem. Something about the guard was familiar, a reflection of someone he had known before, or a spirit he had seen. There was more that drifted beneath the surface of this particular mortal heart.

And try as he might, Apollo could not discern the depths of the man's intentions.

CHAPTER 16

Rennear had been young, eight perhaps. His mother had died a few months before. He still missed her almost every moment of the day.

"It is time to put this behind you, Rennear Ignatius," his father said. "You must step into your future. Come."

Father turned on his heel and marched out of the room. Rennear's caretaker, a kind, elderly woman, bit her lip to stop its tremble, tears brimming in her eyes. "Run along, little master," she said. "Do as your father says."

Several months would pass before he saw her again, after the change.

Rennear sprinted down the hall, his breath shallow in his chest. If he had already lost sight of Father . . . he sighed. The long black cloak swished around the corner ahead. He picked up his pace and soon was hurrying along at his father's side.

His thoughts whirled as they walked—where were they headed? Were they going to visit Mother's grave again? His breath caught. He'd left the flowers he'd picked for her back in his room. "Father, I—"

"Now is the time for listening, son. A great deal of work has gone into what you are about to witness." They wound down into the lower floors of the house. Four armed guards stood before a large wooden door. They bowed at his father's approach. A few moments passed as they unbarred the door. Two followed after him and Father as they marched down a dark stone hall.

Rennear wished he could hold his mother's hand. The darkness had taken her away from him. He'd awakened in the middle of the night, gripped by a terrible dream, and run to her room. But he was too late. The sickness, brought on by the dark, had already claimed her.

He clenched his small hands into fists. Father wouldn't understand. He would be disappointed and tell Rennear that future senators were not afraid of the dark.

Yelps and screams echoed up from below. Rennear gasped and clutched his father's cloak. To his surprise, Father placed a hand on his back. "Come along, son."

Torchlight gleamed in the tunnel ahead. They passed empty cells reinforced with doors of iron, and the frightening sounds grew louder. Beneath the cries, the gnashing and growls of wolves surrounded Rennear.

One of the guards came to stand beside him as they stopped. His father glared down at Rennear, but the kind guard next to him reached down for his hand. "There's a good lad. These beasts won't hurt you."

Rennear gripped the man's hand, and they continued on.

The tunnel opened onto a sunken arena, brightly lit with glowing torches all around.

Along the sandy floor, armed guards stood with bloody pikes, shoving chained lines of men forward. The captives shook, and many shut their eyes, the dirt on their faces streaked with dried blood and meandering paths of tears.

Rennear cried out in fright, and the guard scooped him up, carrying him forward. On the opposite side of the arena, a pack of werewolves gathered, hunched and snarling. A man clad in thick furs, the hide of a gray wolf, stood tall at the center of their pack. He carried a crooked wooden staff and nothing more.

At his nod, the guards in the arena shoved the next pair of prisoners forward. The men fell to their knees, and two werewolves darted toward them, shoulder muscles bulging, and sank their teeth into the base of the men's necks. They screamed in pain. A second nod, and another group of werewolves loped forward, dragging the men off with jaws clamped tight around thighs and feet.

They pulled the stricken men to the edges of the arena where tunnels led off into darkness in a system that stretched across the depths of the city. But even before they reached the passages, their cries had given way to a shaking illness that racked their bodies. Their eyes rolled back in their heads. And then the darkness claimed them.

"This is my life's work, Rennear," Father said, gazing down at the arena. "Too many members of the council are weak, unwilling to embrace the greatness of Andel-ce Hevra's destiny. But not I. The Pantheon Supreme smiles down on House Ignatius, my son. You and I will rise to heights of which my father and his father could have hardly dreamt."

The fur-clad man in the arena looked up at them then. He barked a command, and the werewolves stilled. They rested on their back haunches, large shoulders turned in, bodies erect, almost like a line of Father's soldiers. "Senator Ignatius," the large man growled. He clapped his arm to his chest and bowed his head. The pack of werewolves dipped their snouts, rising with the man. "The hunt is strong, my friend."

Father smiled. "And growing stronger, Talax."

The large man called one of the werewolves forward, and the creature rapidly transformed. The werewolf lifted a fur covering from a pile to the side and draped it around his bare waist. Talax handed him the staff and strode across the center of the arena. He climbed a narrow stone ladder and vaulted over the wall at the top. Talax bowed a second time and gestured for Father to lead the way.

Below, the transformation ritual resumed.

Senator Ignatius guided the guards, Rennear, and Talax through a second set of winding tunnels. Flat, glowing eyes shone out from the depths of the prison cells that lined the sides. Every now and again, a trapped werewolf lunged at the iron bars. Rennear clung tighter to the guard who carried him.

The passageway opened onto a smaller arena with only one iron door embedded in the stone wall of its base. Father inclined his head toward the arena door. "Go get her." Talax and the second guard banged their arms against their chests and climbed down into the arena.

With a look from his father, the guard carrying Rennear set him down. Father bent his knee onto the stone floor and placed his hands on Rennear's shoulders. "A powerful servant of the Pantheon Supreme has warned me of a great evil that will soon come into being on the other side of the world, much like the evil empress who once subjugated our citizens. The city looks to men like us to protect them. We must begin to prepare now to keep our people safe from this looming threat."

Rennear nodded. "And that's why you have the werewolves here, Father? Are they going to help us? I thought they hurt people." He shuddered at the echoes of the screams still ringing in his ears.

Father shook his head. "Some werewolves, ones in the wild, do hurt people. But I have forged an alliance with Talax and his pack. They will be our allies and do as I bid. Would I let them hurt people who didn't deserve it?"

He scrunched his face at this question. "N-no, Father. You wouldn't." What had the men in chains done to be sentenced to being turned into werewolves? It must have been very evil. He had always heard that werewolves were dangerous and cruel, but if Father said they were their friends . . . And Talax had behaved like many of the other soldiers did toward his father. Maybe Rennear had misunderstood.

A girl's scream tore through the chamber. Rennear gasped and looked around. The fierceness of her cry said that she was in trouble.

"Rennear." Father gripped his shoulders tighter. "It is time for you to be brave now."

What was Father saying? "I don't—"

"Like all forms of power, alliances come with a cost. Talax and I forged an arrangement between the city and his pack. He also follows the servant of the Pantheon Supreme who aids my work in the council. Wolves, and werewolves, follow an alpha. The old alpha of his pack was evil. I slew him myself." Father rolled his shoulders back, a smirk tugging at his lip. "This left Talax in charge of the werewolves, much like a captain of the guard. Like Captain Gustaf here." Father gestured to the man who had carried Rennear through the tunnels. "Don't you want to be like him?"

Rennear nodded. "Yes, Father." He smiled up at the captain. He wanted to be brave and helpful.

The man gave a grim nod in return. His brows were knit; they hadn't been before.

Another cry from the girl reached Rennear. He turned, but Father seized his chin. "I knew you did, Rennear. Now, I need you to do something for me. And for your mother's memory."

"Anything, Father."

"The beast you hear is the last remaining child of the alpha. If allowed to live, it will try to turn the werewolves against us, which will put all of our people in danger. Is that something you want?"

Rennear hadn't heard a beast. He had only heard a girl. Was the beast threatening her? Father wasn't making sense. Why would they wait so long to help her? Rennear didn't know what to say.

The metal door of the arena clanged open. Talax emerged, pushing a struggling young woman in front of him, his grip tight on her arms. Thin, dirty rags barely covered her body. Rennear looked away, but Father rose and clamped his hand on Rennear's head, twisting him back to face the arena. The girl was older than he'd thought, in her early teens, but very thin. She tried again to wrench herself free of Talax's grasp, but he was too strong. The large werewolf murmured something in her ear. He threw his head back and laughed. Her large brown eyes darted around the chamber until they landed on Rennear and his father.

Rennear had never seen eyes blaze with such hatred before, but her gaze glowed. She gnashed her teeth then, snarling. Her canines lengthened.

Father grinned and held out his hand toward Captain

Gustaf. The man withdrew a dagger from the bandolier strapped to his chest, and Father knelt once more and tucked the dagger into Rennear's hand. "It's up to you, son. Will you do what it takes to protect our people?"

His mouth fell open. Surely Father could not be asking him to slaughter this girl. Her growls rose up all around him, shaking the walls alongside Talax's laughter.

"Climb down, son." Father pushed him toward the stone stair, and Rennear walked over slowly. Father and Captain Gustaf followed.

He turned at the base of the stairs to survey the arena as his fighting masters had taught him. Talax stood smiling. A small but fully transformed werewolf writhed in his arms. "At your command, Senator."

Father nodded.

In a whirl of fur, the young woman tore free from Talax and leapt at the guard beside him. The man screamed and fell to the ground, clutching his neck. Rennear froze. He had practiced sword fighting in the training yard, but nothing like this. The metal blades he had used before were blunted or covered.

The dagger in his hand gleamed bright silver.

A silvered blade for killing werewolves.

The werewolf spun away from the fallen guard, snarling at Rennear. She rushed forward.

Still he could not move.

"Captain." Father's voice was low and even.

The captain stepped forward between the sprinting werewolf and Rennear, blocking her path. She lunged, clawing and biting until she found a weak spot in his armor near his elbow.

Captain Gustaf cried out and fell to the ground.

The werewolf girl's dark eyes darted back and forth between Rennear and Father.

"Rennear, it's time."

At Father's words, the girl's slathering jaws spread wide in a grin. She twisted in the sand and bounded toward the senator.

Mother had been so cold when he found her. The women who helped her, who had been by her side through her long sickness, held one another and sobbed. Rennear had curled up beside her and cried, holding her hand and begging her to come back to him, to not leave him alone.

The healers had pried his hands loose, and Father had stood, stern and stricken, by the door. His jaw twinged as they carried her body from the room.

They'd covered her casket in blue flowers.

He couldn't lose Father too.

Rennear threw himself into the girl's side, knocking them both to the ground. She sprang to her feet and howled in rage. Rennear crawled away as she stalked nearer. He'd dropped the shining dagger just out of reach.

In a single bound, she landed on top of his chest, pinning him against the sand. Her saliva speckled over his face, and a red glow shone behind her eyes.

The wild evil Father had spoken of.

Her jaw clamped down on his neck, and Rennear screamed in pain.

A soft hiss above him, and her jaw slackened. The werewolf's body toppled to the side as Father withdrew his sword.

Solid footsteps stomped nearer, and a brawny arm wrapped around Rennear's waist and pulled him away. Talax held him tight to his chest.

Father scooped Rennear's discarded silver dagger from

the sand and sank it deep into the werewolf girl's heart. "I will free you and your people from this weakness, Talax," he said. Father withdrew the silvered blade with a flourish. "And from the tyranny of the moons."

The girl lay still, her blood staining the surrounding sand.

Father rose, fixing his gaze on his son. "This is your destiny, Rennear. You will lead elite troops the likes of which this city has never before seen. A true alpha. Talax will show you the way."

Rennear's body convulsed as the lycanthropy took hold. His head slammed back, jarring his senses. "Father!" he screamed.

But Father walked away across the sand.

"Fear not, little master," the werewolf holding him growled, "the moons have much to show you. And then, you will lead a pack all your own."

CHAPTER 17

"WHERE ROOTS REMAIN"

As Cassandra taught us, we retell the stories that first bound our destiny. These stories make us her chosen people. Their telling reaffirms who we are.

In one of these first stories, a young saudad lost her mother at too early an age. The two alone of their muster escaped Orison's fall, the city's destruction claiming their family's tragic fate. It was all the mother could do to see her daughter safely to shore. She hid her inside an ancient forest, its wisdom vast, its canopy great.

Though the child could never have known it then, Cassandra smiled upon her still. It is a truth we hold dear to heart—the goddess of fate abandons us not. No saudad walks the worlds on their own.

The goddess called upon souls nearby to join the young saudad. Spirits of the earth wept with the girl, and the waters trembled, edging near.

The air alone knew what to do.

Gentle breezes awakened faery spirits and sent them to the girl's side. They drifted around her, holding aloft glowing orbs of colorful light. "Come away with us," they called.

But the girl, set adrift on her internal sea, refused their invitation. "I cannot leave my mother's spirit here alone," she said.

One by one, the faeries nodded. "We will come back for you tomorrow."

As each new evening saw its dawn, the faeries returned, carrying dusk on flitting wings. "You will come away with us today," they sang.

But the girl again declined. "Who beyond myself will watch over her grave?" She had not yet heard of the spirits of the earth, wind, and trees.

The faery chorus knew of a verdant land where the saudad's spirit could revive and renew. There they would teach her their magic and stories. There they would share what they knew.

Whatever the girl had chosen for herself, they could not leave her to such a bleak and lonely fate.

As she again turned down their offer, the heart of the youngest faery was the first to break. "How are we to show her a world she does not know?" the faery wondered aloud.

Her question flickered across the anxious faces of her fluttering friends. Such small beings, their hearts resting high, just beneath the coverings of their chests.

"She is right," the others cried. One by one, they flew away. Tempered moonlight and the stars cast their glow upon their wings.

The girl looked up as the flutter ceased. One small faery, the one who had spoken first, remained. "Why do you wait here with me?" asked the girl. The sharp edge of hurt glittered in her tone.

"Because no one should have to mourn alone."

For three days, the faery sat by the girl's side as she tended to her mother's grave. "She was the boss of our muster," the girl explained. "She carried our courage, our destination, in her heart."

As dusk returned in deep orange light, a flower rose from the surface of the earthen mound.

The girl's eyes were wide as she addressed her faery friend. "What do you think it means?"

"We shall see," the faery replied. For though she knew, the truth was for the girl's heart to descry.

As the days continued on, the saudad added garlands to her mother's earth-covered tomb. Each day, the flower blossomed, petals outstretching into bloom.

Your mother's spirit speaks, the faery longed to say. *She knows the hearts of earth and sea, of sky and trees, and seeks to share them with you.*

A quiet wisdom stilled the faery's words with a melody all its own—*Understanding comes with time. It needs a chance to grow.*

Every winter finds its spring, as so many stories show. The same was true for this our tale, of girl and faery, love and woe.

In time, the saudad came to perceive the unique offerings nature made, how each carried her mother's cherished memory. Their times on horseback returned on the fragrant breeze. Her welcoming arms that pulled her daughter along on adventures were traced in the delicate, angling reach of the trees. And by the brook, the way her mother laughed as she sang echoed back to the girl. Finally, the earth's embrace, which now cradled her mother's body, returned the girl to herself, her mooring reattained.

"Do you miss your faery friends?" she asked her companion one day.

"Of course I do." The faery smiled. "I have ever since they went away. But something compelled me to stay by your side—"

"So that I would not mourn alone?"

"Yes," the faery continued, "but it was more than such a sense on its own." Her tiny features contorted, scowling bark, furious wings. "We have so much more to show you," she said. "The world is richer still than it seems."

A single tear fell from the girl's eye as she looked back upon her mother's grave. "Go now, cher'a," she heard her mother say, "you carry my spirit with you, on this and every day." The magic flower then lifted her head and stretched up to the sky. "Take me with you, as a sign. We all must live and die."

Her hand trembled as she cupped the fragile flower in her palm. "But there is no need for you to die today."

"With the two of us together," the faery carefully said, "she continues to live on."

The girl sighed and ever so carefully plucked the flower at her stem.

Bright red blossoms shuddered. They opened and closed—and she heard the flower's voice again. "Still I blossom, still I bloom, so long as my roots remain. Go along from here, sweet saudad child. Inside your heart, dwells always your domain."

Girl and faery took up the floral song as they walked over field and fen. From this great loss, love and stories did their work—they offered healing to those who remained.

CHAPTER 18

Cerdris ran his fingers through his hair. "Hold on, Persephonie," he said, scowling at the storyteller on the opposite side of the table, "so are you saying that Faela was or wasn't in love with Meris?" Persephonie had spent the last hour setting up the love between a saudad man and a fae who stood at crossed fates only for the fae to turn from her love for a different path.

"Both." She stared back at him as if this response was completely expected instead of falling outside the norms of every story he had heard and loved. Persephonie giggled at his confusion and took another sip of her wine. "Faela loved Meris, but in her heart, she loved her forest more, and it was her forest who truly needed her."

He thumped his forearms onto the tabletop. "That's it? Her forest needs her more, so she sacrifices herself for the forest and never sees Meris again?"

"No, of course not." Persephonie sighed and shook her head, adopting an exasperated expression she seemed to have plucked straight from Tess. She scrunched her lips together, mulling over how best to explain the gaps in the story to him. "Let us try this way. Competing loves are not difficult to understand, are they?"

He shook his head. "They're relatively common in most storytelling traditions."

Persephonie pointed her finger at him. "Perhaps that is the problem." She continued before he could object. "You want each story to fit neatly into a place beside other stories, as though they make up one single tapestry that you could visit, or like they could be crammed together in a library or something." She leaned back and crossed her arms, her eyes narrowly focused as though she evaluated an invisible masterpiece. "But stories do not work that way." Her abrupt tone dissipated the illusion.

She drummed her fingers against her lips. "Alright, Cassandra would explain it like this—*we* are the tapestry, and the stories are the threads. We exist inside of them, not the other way around."

Cerdris frowned. That wasn't possible—

Persephonie grinned at his doubt. "I do not know what more to tell you that will help you to believe me beyond that one day, you will see." She shrugged and slid out of the booth. "I need to see if Tess needs help in the back before I leave."

"Hmm, as you wish, Mistress Persephonie." Now he was the one imitating one of Tess's gestures, in this case, their dubious eye-roll. "Enjoy the concert tonight," he called after her. Only a few weeks in the city, and already she had caught the attention of the captain of the guard, Patron Ignatius.

Her long hair swung over her shoulder as she glanced back at him. "Oh, I will." He could have sworn the tavern lights flared around her when she smiled.

Cerdris lifted his goblet, toasting her and her exciting

evening. Tess would be along in a few minutes to refill his glass, and then he would need to hide for an hour or so before Patron Ignatius arrived. Though he had promised Otmund he wouldn't, he was determined to ensure that Persephonie wasn't about to fall into a trap of some sort designed by the patron's father. Otmund had mentioned that Persephonie and her mother had ties to the Untamed, which meant that any mixing with the senator's son was dangerous at best, fatal—or more—at worst.

Two hours later, he peered out from behind the bushes as the black coach slowed to a stop in front of the Green Owl. Seeing the patron up close, Cerdris thought Persephonie's lack of caution made more sense, but still. There were plenty of handsome men in Andel-ce Hevra. He had met several last week alone—

Persephonie laughed as she traipsed after Patron Ignatius, who gallantly handed her into the carriage and sprang in after her. With the sharp *thwack* of the reins, the carriage rolled away across the cobblestones.

That was that, and what had he to show for his snooping aside from a throbbing in his left knee from squatting in the dirt for too long?

Ten paces away from the tavern, Cerdris whirled around, alerted by the sound of an overturned pebble behind him. Persephonie's fox, Juliet, stared up at him with wide amber eyes, her head tilted to the side.

"Hello there." He mimicked the gesture. "Should you be out here on your own?"

Juliet bounded away down a side street, and Cerdris called out in alarm, chasing after her as best he could in his worn leather shoes. *Add new soles to the list of things to replace once Drugas gets back to me about the advance.* Surely the guard had received news of his find by now . . .

Cerdris skidded to a stop and rested his hand against his chest as Juliet spun in a circle at the end of the alley. "What're you after, foxy?" He frowned and crouched down, pulling his breeches up to grant his thighs more space. His left knee twinged at being once again subjected to this cramped position.

"Mewl," Juliet yawn-cried at him. Even after their fourth storytelling session together, he couldn't understand the fox's sounds or expressions without Persephonie's help.

"Wouldn't you like to come with me?" He opened his arms wide, inviting Juliet into his embrace. Otmund would undoubtedly be irritated at seeing him return so soon after he had promised to leave earlier that afternoon, but why would he be so quick to turn away one of his favorite patrons? And returning the fox was a perfect excuse. Would Otmund believe Juliet had found him?

The alley shadows deepened, and a hush fell, as though he had suddenly ducked his head below water. A low, rumbling voice spoke from the sudden shadows. "*Like* isn't quite the word I would use, no."

CHAPTER 19

Persephonie leaned her head against Rennear's shoulder as the carriage took them through the dark city streets. Her stomach still fluttered at the memory of his lips pressed to hers during the magical mermaid song. Their kiss was a different intimacy from the story he had shared the night before, a picture of his past that he had entrusted into her keeping. She held the fragile butterfly in her hand, clutched closely against the light of her heart.

With his hand wrapped around her hip, he had led her through the crowd to his carriage. Rennear handed her in and directed the coachmen to one of the private parks in City Central. Lamplight flickered across the windows as they rode. He held her hand in his lap as she gazed over the sleeping city. The mermaid's music drifted through her mind, punctuated by the staccato clomping of the horses' hooves.

"Are you sure that we can go to this park, Rennear? My mother warned me away from it on one of my first visits here as a child. I was following a butterfly, and she stopped me just before the guards did."

He traced the back of her hand with his thumb. "You can go anywhere in the city that you want whenever you're with me."

"But I will still be me there." The werewolves' attack in the alley behind Otmund's pub sat heavy in the silence between them.

Rennear leaned closer. His bronze eyes flared as they passed a street lantern. "And that is precisely why I want to be wherever you are."

Their breath mingled. Persephonie closed the space between them, pressing her lips, her chest, her stomach into his. Rennear held her tight against him, and she wrapped her arms around the back of his neck.

He groaned as the carriage slowed and came to a stop. Rennear pulled his mouth away from hers. His lips spread into a wide smile as he sighed, running his fingers through her hair. "I should have picked a park that was farther away." He cleared his throat and sat up straight before sweeping into a mock-formal bow. "Fair mistress Persephonie, if you would do me the honor."

She giggled and accepted his proffered hand. "Yes, I will."

Rennear led her out of the carriage and onto the cobblestone street. He reached back inside behind her and withdrew a black silk shawl embroidered with tiny flowers and leaves. "Just in case." He unfolded the shimmering fabric with a flourish, refolded it in a triangle, and draped it around her shoulders. Braided fringe hung from the edges and tickled her arms.

"Do you keep this in your carriage for evenings at the

park?" The edges of the embroidered flowers caught on her fingertips as she ran her hands over the silk.

"Not usually, no." Rennear tucked his arm around her shoulder and led her toward the archway that marked the park's entrance. "But I saw it at the market earlier today, and it made me think of you."

She leaned her head against him, angling her face up toward his as they walked. "It's lovely. Thank you."

The cut-stone wall gave way to an intricate metal archway whose pattern resembled the braided fringe of her new shawl. Two guards stepped out of the shadows, hands upheld to tell them to halt, but they lowered their arms when they recognized Rennear. "Patron Ignatius." They each clamped a fist to their chest and bowed.

"Apologies, sir," the one on the left said.

Rennear nodded to both of them. "Thank you. I know it is after hours, but might my companion and I take a turn about the Empress's Gardens?"

"Of course, sir." They bowed again and stepped back. The second guard set about opening the gate. The hinges whispered, and the bottom of the gate scraped over the pebbled pathway. "Will you be requiring a lantern, Patron Ignatius?"

Persephonie shook her head against his shoulder. Rennear glanced down, the side of his mouth twisted in a small smile. "I believe the moons and stars grant us enough light this evening."

"Very well, sir."

She and Rennear slipped beneath the sweeping boughs of the trees that lined the garden path. As they walked, the tiny pebbles crunched against one another beneath her slippers. "Why did you call this the Empress's Garden?" She knew that the council reserved the elegant parks for the city's nobility and political servants, but she'd never heard it attributed to the exiled empress before.

"Ah, that is one of many interesting quirks of Andel-ce Hevran history." Rennear turned her from the path lined with flowering trees to one lined with tulips. Beyond the carefully planted rows of flowers was a sweeping meadow that held three sprawling elms. The tulip buds were closed tight, lips concealing a secret they desperately wished to reveal.

Rennear adopted their conspiratorial air, his voice dipping and diving over the winding edges of the story. "According to the legend, after the priests, generals, and senators who would later form the Council of Andel-ce Hevra drove the evil druidic empress and her monsters from the city, they set about torching each of the empress's beloved gardens, razing them to the ground." His eyes flashed with the drama of his story, but he paused to ensure she had caught the overexaggeration of both the honor he placed upon the Council and the sneering condemnation he affected when referring to the empress.

"And then what?" Persephonie whispered, eager for him to continue. Before they'd met, a city servant speaking of evil druidic magic would have made her feel hurt as well as frightened, but now, after Rennear had shared his secret with her, and after their evening together, the accusation didn't hold the power over her that it would have. She knew its false nature with every spark of her being, and she knew that Rennear did too. Perhaps this garden held a secret for understanding the empress and why the city continued to hate her—as if the empress still frightened them.

"We shall reclaim these spaces for the people of our great city." Rennear thrust his fist into the air, pretending to be one of the famous Andel-ce Hevran generals from the years following the great flood. "Trees were burned, shrubs fashioned to resemble animals of all shapes and sorts were maimed, flowers were uprooted and tossed onto garbage heaps." Rennear sighed and glanced over his shoulder. He took both of her hands and guided her over the row of tulips and toward the third elm tree. Rennear covered her eyes for the last several steps, holding her against his chest as he led her to the tree's trunk. He turned her around, leaning her back against the rough bark. The stubble of his beard scratched the side of her ear. "We should wait for the clouds to pass."

His lips met hers in the darkness. She kept her eyes closed, pinned between him and the sacred tree. Countless stories wound around the roots of the elm, weaving about her and Rennear now and holding them tight in their embrace. To the saudad, it was a guardian tree, symbolic of the wide wings of Apollo. Rennear's heart pounded against her hand. She ground the other into the gray-green bark of the tree. His breath hitched as her palm drifted lower down his chest. He pulled her hips closer to his.

The druids held that the elm was powerful enough to maintain a lover's bond, even after the beloved had journeyed on to Astralei. "There's a reason the elm graces both the card for THE LOVERS and for DEATH, Persephonie," Mama had said.

Rennear pulled away suddenly. He caught her hands and held them close against his chest. They both breathed quickly. Rennear didn't take his eyes from her. Behind him, a silver glow bathed the branches of the elm. It reflected against his skin. "And then they came to this garden," he whispered. "Here, for just a moment, everything changed."

The silver gleam grew brighter as they rounded the

wide trunk of the tree, shining through the sweeping branches of the elm. Persephonie gasped. Behind the gateway tree was a hillside covered in argent maples. They shone pure silver, basking in the light of the moons. She stopped, staring. Never before had she seen so many of the trees blessed by the lunar goddess Selene all in one place. Their collective radiance was as bright as a third moon, hung low in the gardens, coating her and Rennear in their light. "I can hardly believe it."

His eyes shone in the treelight, sweeping from her to their glowing leaves and back. "Will you walk beneath their branches with me?"

Wordlessly, Persephonie nodded.

Beneath the boughs, the ivory light took on a liquid weight, painting their skin as though they'd stood still in a silver rain. She ran her finger over the ridges of a leaf, the blood in her veins arcing toward the tree's lunar energy. "After seeing this, they still wanted to destroy the gardens?"

Rennear's brow creased. "The way my mother told it, this was the last garden left. Many of the priests fell to their knees along the hillside, weeping at what they had done. The generals bowed. They saw the argents' proximity to the elms as a symbol of their fallen soldiers, the ones who had passed through the portal of death into the wide waters of the astral seas." His shoulders lowered, and he stared at the earth beneath their feet, thick blades of grass, white in the light of the trees. "But the senators, they knew what to do." He ran his hand back through his hair. His jaw clenched. Finally, he took her hand again. "'We'll make it a private garden,' they said. 'For the elite and their families, so we always remember the cost of the empress's rule, what *she* took from the city, and the mercy, the restraint we showed in that which we spared.'"

He had spoken of his mother a little before. Persephonie knew she had died when he was young. In those early years of her son's life, from what she could tell, his mother had planted the seeds that would blossom into questions against his father's strict tenets, the limiting beliefs through which Senator Ignatius and those like him framed their world.

"We have a story about the argent trees, Rennear." Legends served as water over scattered seeds, bringing to the surface the truths that lay buried beneath.

He kissed the flat planes of her knuckles. "Tell it to me."

She smiled and pulled him deeper into the argent forest. "Like all the best stories, this legend, taught to us by Cassandra, is a story of love." He raised his eyebrows, waiting for her to continue. "It can be easy to forget, in the darknesses that cover the world, but this plane, and all of the others, they came to be out of the forces of love."

Persephonie took a deep breath, sinking into the lulling rhythm of her people's stories. "It is love that binds, just as love divides." His hand traced the line of her waist, sparking butterflies in her stomach, but she pulled away out of reach, not allowing him to distract her from her tale, not yet. "Many have forgotten, and many more know not how to see. My datha says it is up to us, the saudad, to remind and teach them, those who are ready to remember. And for the rest, we hold this knowledge dear until they too yearn to no longer forget."

She spun, walking backward until she reached the trunk of one of the silver trees. Rennear's arms and the tree's branches pinned her in on either side.

"And which legend is this, story mistress of the saudad?" Rennear tucked a curled strand of hair behind her ear.

"We call this one 'The Legend of Enidia.' It recounts the great, long-lasting love of two ancient trees in the worlds' first forests. An argent maple, lunar bearer of the skies above, and her lover, the elm, guardian of the worlds of death below." She held a finger to his lips as he leaned closer.

CHAPTER 20

"THE LEGEND OF ENIDIA"

As Cassandra taught us, love and its stories exist in many forms. Countless peoples have forgotten this truth in a tradition that dates back even to the earliest days of the world. Pursuing their own ends, these civilizations separated those who should not have been, those who loved one another, who held deep lore and love all their own.

One such story comes to us on the whispers borne between the boughs. It tells of a love from those earliest years, where deep in the forest, spirit intertwined between argent maple and her lover elm.

"Jasper." Enidia exhaled the name in the early morning air.

He awoke beside her.

"By the light," he said with a warm wave of pollen.

"By the light," she answered with a flurry of her own.

They shared breakfast together, a flirtatious exchange between intertwined roots.

It had been she who initiated their friendship. One morning, in early spring. She stopped growing toward him, granting him full access to the light.

He answered with generosity in turn and fed her a share of the nutrients gifted him by the sun.

Out of these simple gestures, trees' great loves are born.

One day, a young woman walked by. She spoke to the two trees and smiled at their response. They told stories together. She fell asleep atop their roots, and they sheltered her from the midnight rain as best they could.

The next morning, the young woman awoke. "Would you like to come with me?"

"This is our home," Jasper answered.

"But I'm scared to continue through the forest alone."

"There is nothing here to be frightened of," Enidia assured her.

"I have always loved argent maples," the girl said. She murmured something under her breath.

Enidia's body tingled. Pain shot up and down her trunk, across branches and leaves, down through her roots, as though she'd caught fire. Though they shared much, she tried to shield Jasper from whatever curse the girl had uttered, to protect him from the bolts of pain.

His panic drifted toward her—dry, bitter, urgent. "Enidia!" he called. The scents of desperation.

The cry originated from her heart core, and Enidia fell. She tumbled, trunk split asunder from the roots, branches quaking in her and Jasper's shared sunlight before they crashed to the ground.

Her screams echoed across the forest, ricocheting back to her.

The earth caught her as she fell.

But the sky did not fall sideways as it should have.

Jasper's branches held her up. The warm scent of wonder fell in soft drips on her face. "Enidia?"

The space near a small branch, one she had grown only recently, parted. The girl stood beside her, smiling. Jasper held her in a circle of branches. He was so . . . tall.

"My darling," Jasper whispered. Too many smells lingered on the breeze. What did he mean? She reached out for him with her roots as she had so often done. But there was nothing but the soft press of earth beneath.

Her towering love beside her . . . there was suddenly so much of him she could not perceive. Only the lowest branches and a solid stretch of trunk.

Enidia's own trunk and branches had been . . . softened by the fall. She gasped at the sudden press of the air all around her—and she echoed the wisping sound of the wind, not the distinguished groan of a tree.

Beside Jasper, the trunk and limbs where she had been leaned, a hole gouged in her side as if by lightning's strike.

His rain of pollen continued. She felt and understood so little. Her body she perceived of its own accord and not in relation to those nearby, her friends, Jasper . . . Only four of her branches remained. A short, spindly one on either side, and two where her trunk should have been.

Jasper's branches helped her to balance as she swayed side to side.

"What have you done?" Enidia demanded.

"I've rescued you," the girl said. "You're free now."

Jasper stood. Frozen. Silent.

"Come on." The girl reached out her hand for Enidia's branches. "You're the prettiest one I've made yet."

"There are more?" Though she couldn't feel it, Enidia knew her heart matched Jasper's, petrified as stone.

The girl tugged at her branches, and Enidia stumbled forward. Her limbs slipped free of Jasper's, his bark somehow rough.

She did not turn away from him as the girl pulled her through the forest. Her love's branches stretched wide and tall, reaching out for her, calling her back. Half of him was missing, hidden by the earth. Still, she knew he called for her. His pollen clung to her softened bark, though for the first time, she could not hear his voice.

Enidia called back to him, a bird's cry lost on the breeze. The girl continued to yank at her branches. They entered a part of the forest Enidia didn't know.

"There is much that I can teach you," the girl told her on that sunlit afternoon. She told Enidia how to identify the parts of herself that had separated from her body. A different body. Head. Arms. Legs. The girl called her form "dryad."

Seasons passed.

Many of the others were as heartbroken as she. Some had forgotten themselves entirely.

No matter how often the girl said it, Enidia knew they were not free.

The girl gathered more dryads around her. She made her own grove of severed trees.

Even the dryads who had forgotten themselves, who had forgotten the forests from which they came, grew concerned. "Why do you gather so many of us?" they asked the girl.

"Because one day they will come for me," the girl said with a shake of her head. "And I don't intend to be taken again."

The dryads did not know of whom she spoke.

Enidia watched and waited. The girl's magic grew in might. She returned with more severed sister trees.

And one day, the promised danger arrived.

To Enidia, the newcomers didn't look very different from the girl. They strode confidently on branch-legs. But instead of the glisten of magic at their fingertips, they carried shiny weapons instead.

"What have we here?" one with a deep voice said to the girl.

"Witch!" "Enchantress!" the others sneered.

Enidia didn't know what they meant by the words that they used, but the girl snarled back at them. "You've no idea whom you've stumbled upon." She called white fire from her fingertips, and lightning flashed overhead. "By the light!" the girl screamed.

In an instant, the dryads nearest her fell dead. Their spirits swirled forth from their trunks, transformed from verdant life to the brilliant fire the girl wielded. She swept her arm from hip to shoulder, and the white flame burned across the strangers' chests. The first line of strangers and their silver weapons toppled over onto the earth. Those who had come behind cried out and ran toward the girl.

"By the light," she yelled again.

Above, the sky darkened. Only the two moons remained in the sudden dusk. Their light shone on Enidia.

A second circle of dryads fell. Their spirits, too, flew forward at the girl's whim.

But around Enidia, misty shadows clung. They carried with them a protective pollen, and a whisper—Jasper's— that years had passed since she had heard.

With the girl's third casting of the spell, the remaining dryads fell.

Their spirits drifted up toward the moons. The girl slashed forward with her hands.

Shadows clung to the dryads' spirits. They trickled back as rain onto the ground.

The girl gasped and spun toward Enidia. She cast her spell once more.

Roots groaned deep beneath the earth, and a wall of shadow rose. Wide-reaching branches encircled Enidia. They absorbed the girl's spell.

"Impossible," she whispered.

Like the first lashing of a thunderstorm, the remaining strangers surged forth. Their silver weapons thunked into the girl.

By nightfall, Enidia stood alone inside the clearing. Beads of white dribbled from the bodies of her sister-dryads. Their spirits swirled, guided by root and shadow back into the earth.

"Wait below until one who is worthy calls you," Enidia whispered as they returned to the world beneath. The earth would hold their souls, their stories, and remember. And for this memory, this story is told.

With her sisters laid to rest, Enidia returned home, walking back the way she had come.

She followed a trail of pollen and the whisper-groans of the roots that lay hidden, stretching into worlds dark and vast, far below.

Jasper exhaled relief when she returned. "I have been waiting for you," he said. A breeze blew, and she turned to her former trunk.

Thick moss grew up the sides, and many branches were bare that should not have been.

"I did my best to keep you alive and with me," Jasper said. His voice was tired.

She smelled moss on him too. A new kind. He was sick.

"Were you able to keep me nearby?" Enidia asked.

He chucked sadly on the breeze. "Not well."

She stepped forward till their trunks touched. Enidia ran her arm branches down his sides and trailed her leaves over his.

"You protected me, that day, from the girl."

"I did, my love." Jasper held his limbs still.

"I do not know if I can return to my trunk . . ."

A shudder of pollen fell from above. "Then join me in mine."

Enidia leaned her palm against his bark.

Jasper accepted her with a sigh of surprise. There, inside the shelter of his trunk, he waited, the same as he had always been. He wrapped one arm around her waist. With the other, he traced the line of her face with the tip of a finger, held her close, and brought her lips to his.

Later, Enidia would step back into the trunk he had kept alive for her. She would help bring his body and her own back to health. They would smile at the sunlight together and greet one another with warm scents each morning.

But tonight, they explored this new kind of freedom the girl had sentenced them to. Inside Jasper's trunk, the two dryads clung to one another. Roots intertwined. The spaces of their arms, faces, bodies perfectly shared.

And they found it wasn't so different from the freedom they'd known before.

CHAPTER 21

Cerdris froze as a single silhouette separated from the stretched shapes in the alley before him. A towering devil of some kind, with horned wings that spread gently in an absent breeze . . .

His hands shook as he slowly turned, his neck craning back to stare at the monster behind him.

"Guardian, human, not monster." The creature clicked his tongue between his teeth. "Shouldn't a writer know the difference?" His golden eyes narrowed at Cerdris before he turned his attention to the fox over his shoulder. "I'm not sure your alarm was justified, Juliet." The guardian raised an eyebrow and motioned the fox closer. "What harm are we anticipating from him?"

Cerdris swallowed a shriek as a large gray hand reached across the space between them, and the guardian poked him in the chest. Juliet trotted to the figure's side.

The guardian nodded as though listening to the fox speak inside his head. "Interesting, interesting. Oh." The golden eyes brightened. "A story thief, is he?" Wide gray lips spread into a crooked grin. "And what have you to say to that, boy?"

"I, umm . . ." Cerdris's breath caught in his throat, only the shallowest wheezes reaching his lungs.

"Well, go on." The guardian leaned closer, and Cerdris's trembling worsened. "How much were you planning to make from Mistress Arelle's stories after you sold them to the guards?"

"I wasn't, uh . . ." Breath screeched through his narrowed throat. Mother had told him stories of the guardians before she passed, but the ones from her tales looked nothing like the black-clad creature before him with a sweeping cape and long, twisted horns.

"Mummy may have omitted a few details," the creature said with a smirk. "Let me finish this sentence you're having such trouble with." He tugged at the elbows of his leather jacket, showing sharp wrist bones between his gloves and sleeve. "You weren't going to share any of your profits with her, were you? Or warn her of the danger you planned to inflict."

Cerdris looked down and shook his head. He needed the money, and with her job for Otmund, with board covered too—

"Do not change the subject." The guardian pressed his fingertip against his temple and closed his eyes. "Have you any notion as to the power, the magic, of Persephonie's stories?"

He shook his head again. Was this creature reading his mind?

"Guardian," the figure growled with a lunging step forward.

Cerdris cried out and fell back onto his hands. His

right wrist struck the stone. The impact lurched up his arm and clamped his jaw shut.

The guardian drew himself up tall once more and straightened the waist of his jacket. "Apollo, to be precise, one of five." He swept into a low bow. "Had you behaved differently, you and I might be on the same side." The sideways smirk returned. "But I cannot abide someone trying to cheat one blessed by fate."

"I-I really didn't mean to cheat her," Cerdris stammered. "Persephonie is my friend. She—"

"And *that*," Apollo snarled, "is what makes my task additionally unpleasant as well as why you will be allowed to live, albeit not here. Now, give me the pages."

He couldn't be serious. Was the guardian part of some strange saudad prank that Persephonie had arranged? Or, *gods*. Drugas was calling in his remaining debt early and had arranged an elaborate ruse to scare him into paying.

Apollo chuckled, the sound crackling like ice along Cerdris's bones. "This Drugas you fear has no hold on me, though I wonder if he would be as easy to intimidate as you."

"No, he—"

"That wasn't a question." Apollo waved his hand once more, and the golden orbs of his eyes flared brighter. "Her magic has the power to heal and to kill, to create and destroy, yet you would trade sacred stories for the chance at a few gold coins." The guardian revealed sharpened teeth, the canines overstretched like the fangs of a wolf. "Give your pages to me, and omit none."

Cerdris couldn't breathe as terror gripped his throat. He couldn't surrender them. Doing so would mean—

The golden eyes turned to Persephonie's fox. "Juliet, where are the pages?"

Soft paws poked at his side. *Juliet was trying to help him! No.* A weight lifted from his pocket. The alley's edges grew darker. Still he could not breathe.

"Come, Juliet." Apollo's voice had grown muffled. His boots echoed dully against the cobblestones. "See if you can arrange a note to Persephonie for me, from this false friend of hers."

His pages—weeks of work. He couldn't let this Apollo steal them. Cerdris rolled onto his side, crawling after the towering figure.

"Tsk, tsk, tsk." The guardian's voice faded, replaced by the grating of leather against loose flecks of stone.

A sharp pain at the back of his head as Apollo hoisted his body from the ground by the hair. *What type of magic was this?* He clawed at the straps of leather across Apollo's chest, but his hands weren't working properly. They merely flapped like fish tossed onto the dock.

"I think it will be best for me to remove you from this situation entirely." Apollo's breath rippled in waves of heat over the side of his face, crawling down into his ear.

No, Cerdris tried to shout. His throat made a low, creaking rasp instead. There was nothing beyond the low voice and a distant, gray gold. His vision turned black as the world faded away.

◈

LUCIEN'S GUARDS DRAGGED FORWARD THE SHAKING figure of a beaten werewolf guard, tossing the body at his feet. "The famous Drugas," Lucien drawled, drumming his fingers on the arms of his chair. "Tell me, where are these mystical stories I was promised?"

The guard lifted his head and shoulders, propped by

his elbows on the marble floor. A pool of congealing blood spread beneath him. "I-I can explain, my lord. The writer—"

With a simple flick of his wrist, a whip cracked from the side of the chamber. The guard screamed as the leather struck his flesh.

"My patience is waning." Lucien rose. "Answer my questions directly, and our time together shall be brief."

He took the guard's whimper as assent to the terms. A pity. The ones who fought back were worth sparing. The others . . .

"Do you or do you not have the pages for me?"

The guard had courage enough to look him in the eye. "I do not."

Another wave of his finger. The whip cracked. The guard screamed.

"Do you know the whereabouts of the writer who was to acquire the stories for us and our cause?"

The guard's shoulders shook, and his head drooped down. Gentle sobs racked his body.

"Micaela," Lucien drawled. The shadow tiger padded into the lantern-lit glow, tugging the umbral dark of the Shadowlands with her. "Take our guest below, and see what he remembers."

His tiger growled her eager assent, her black tongue flicking over the soft edges of her lips.

The man's screams echoed throughout the chamber long after Micaela had dragged his broken form from Lucien's sight.

Such a shame.

Lucien returned to his padded chair and rested his rotting face against the soft, scarlet velvet. Perhaps the fault was his—had he missed something along the way? He chuckled to himself as he traced the ivory inlay of the chair. Elusive challenges had a charm of their own.

"This city will still be yours," he whispered to the shadows. In the dark, southern reaches of Azuria, across lands of Shadow and Bright, Alessandra's power grew. He would not fail the goddess. The souls of Andel-ce Hevra, he was certain, would one day soon be hers.

❧

A RATTLING CHAIN WAS THE FIRST TO GREET CERDRIS AS he awoke into a cold, shadowy domain. *"Ach."* He raised his hand to his head, hoping to ease the pounding behind his skull.

The tinging rumble of metal against stone followed his movements.

A sharp breath filled his lungs with dank, stale air. "Where—"

"Welcome to the Court of Apollo," a low, rhythmic voice said out of the darkness around him.

Cerdris's bindings clanked as he spun around. The voice seemed to surround him. His chains came from the floor. Were there no walls here to protect him?

The disembodied voice chuckled. "You will see me soon, as your eyes learn to adjust. But rest assured, I mean you no harm."

"How can I be sure?" Cerdris tried to rub his sore wrists. He winced as the metal dug into his forearms instead.

Jangling chains came nearer. "Very good." The voice lifted somewhat, like a smile. "I see why he selected you."

Selected . . . No, it couldn't be. Had he truly been taken to Apollo's lair? His connections in Andel-ce

Hevra. His debt to Drugas. What would Persephonie think?

"Ah, I have been hearing much of her these last few days."

How could everyone in this shadow-space hear his thoughts and yet he remained blind to them?

"A cruel gift from the guardian, in my case," the voice answered.

Cerdris lowered his head into his hands. He needed to think. To figure out where he was and why. "Who are you?"

The footfalls drew closer, and an armored warrior emerged out of the swirling shadows around him. Dark green eyes narrowed as the warrior took him in. "A figure of legend in saudad stories. One who betrayed the guardian Apollo. A fae cursed with true immortality. One who has known love and loss. Take your pick." The warrior glanced over his armored shoulder.

"I don't understand."

His new companion nodded. "Ah, so you have not yet gleaned all the saudad stories. Or perhaps this is a story Persephonie does not know. Better still, did she keep it from you on purpose, knowing you sold her tales to her enemies?" The warrior slowly turned.

Two curved holes gaped open along the back of the warrior's armor, framing cruel scars between the metal panels covering his shoulder blades.

Cerdris drew back and away with a gasp. What must this figure have endured to sustain such injuries? And enemies . . . what did he mean?

The warrior crouched down in front of Cerdris, just outside his arm's reach. "What indeed, Story-Stealer."

"Wait, I didn't—"

"No. Apollo stopped you."

Cerdris said nothing, waiting as his eyes adjusted to the light. He studied the figure before him.

The warrior's face was equal parts fierce and beautiful. His skin was a deep bronze, a few shades darker than Persephonie's, and the loose strands of his shoulder-length hair played between deepest brown and pure black.

"It is good that you wish to describe me, Story-Stealer."

Cerdris gritted his teeth at the repetition of the name.

"Hmh," the warrior laughed. "Let us return to what you asked me before. I am Emryc, disgraced protector of Circe, the first Chosen of Cassandra."

These names were familiar to him. Persephonie had mentioned them in passing, but she told him of Faela and Meris instead.

A calculating smile spread over half of Emryc's face. "I am glad to see that I am not entirely forgotten." The warrior's dark green gaze flickered over Cerdris. From amid the thick locks of his hair, the pointed tips of bronze fae ears emerged. "Apollo has a new job for you," Emryc continued. "It will grant you a purpose here and, as he says, make supervising you an easier task." Emryc rose and held out his hand. "Come."

The iron chains fell to Cerdris's side with a clatter. Was the warrior setting him free?

Emryc's mirth was deeper this time. "The lord of this realm desires an audience with his story-keeper before you begin your first day of work." He strode into the swirling mist, each step confident, methodical.

Cerdris scrambled to follow after him. His head spun with the first rise to his feet in what must have been days.

He was unfamiliar with this term, story-keeper. And where did Apollo make his court?

"Come along, Story-Stealer," the warrior called over his shoulder. "Fate has smiled upon you." Emryc paused momentarily, glancing back at Cerdris behind him. "You get to record my story first."

CHAPTER 22

"THE FIRST CHOSEN OF CASSANDRA"

Furious shouts and the *tling* of metal sent Circe sprinting down the hall toward the throne room. Their attack wasn't meant to happen for another day. She called upon the river of Cassandra's magic that flowed from deep within. "Let me and Emryc return to the light," she whispered.

Circe gritted her teeth as she slammed her shoulder into the reinforced wooden door, the iron barbs biting her bared skin. She spun into the room, hands raised to shoulder height, magic singing at her fingertips . . . and froze.

The multicolored lanterns that drifted around the room hovered in a circle around the king, Emryc, and Daugath. Fomorian soldiers stood with weapons drawn in a line behind King Lefre. The gemstones in their chests glowed garnet, a sign Daugath had told her to look out for. "It means they are moving into a state of blood fury," he had said. "They'll stop at nothing to fend off the threat to their sovereign."

But it was not the king who was under threat. Circe gasped as she took in the scene before her. Emryc, her warrior, knelt at the feet of the king, his sword kicked away out of his reach. Lefre held the curved blade of an axe against the back of the fae's neck. Opposite the two figures, Daugath's chest heaved, his amethyst gemstone pulsing pale purple light. Out of it, a gentle trickle of violet twirled through the air, drifting toward one of the king's hovering lanterns.

King Lefre's voice boomed out across the throne room. "Our final guest has arrived," he called, raising his gaze toward her with a smile. "I had almost despaired of your making it in time."

"Circe—" Emryc groaned. His warning stopped short as Lefre pressed the axe blade harder against the skin of his neck. The scarlet answer of his blood shone bright in the lantern light.

The king turned his face to the corner of the room and gave a slight nod. Rows of metallic footsteps stomped out of the darkness toward her. She had missed the hidden guards in her eagerness to aid her companions. Emryc's voice from their first years of training together echoed in her mind. "Awareness of your surroundings will save your life. Lack of attention will lose it."

Daugath's head whipped toward her, his bright eyes almost white. They had only a moment to decide their course.

Cassandra help me. Emryc would sacrifice himself to see her freed, she knew as deeply as she held their most sacred stories. And if either she or Daugath attacked the king or his forces now, they would seal Emryc's fate.

The king's deep voice broke through the storm of her thoughts. "While your goddess may not answer, storyteller, I can help you sort through your more pressing questions."

Circe's blood pounded in her ears. *No, no, no, no, no.* She had to do something.

"Answer me this, saudad." The king spoke into the recesses of her mind as Daugath had done in their time in the caves. *"Will you join your two companions on their doomed path, or will you continue in service to me as you were promised?"*

The general had explained how the telepathy worked to some extent, but they'd had little time to practice with so much to plan. A waste, considering how their plan had fallen apart the same night as Emryc's arrival.

"Hold," the king called, his hand raised to the guards who had almost surrounded her.

Their metallic clomping stopped.

"I await your reply," the king said.

"Our thoughts flow like a river through a canyon," Daugath had told her. "The roar of the river may be heard from far above, giving a picture of its breadth and depth. The accuracy of this matters not, for the impression is the same."

Finally, it made sense to her. *As deeply as she knew their most sacred stories . . .*

"Mighty king," Circe cried, striding toward the center of the throne room. The nearest guard seized her around the waist. The force of his grasp drove the breath from her lips, but she swallowed the groan of her bruised ribs.

The lines of Emryc's wings tensed. He was preparing to make a final stand against the king. It would end in his death. Daugath's bleeding gemstone glowed lavender, the same shade as the urns he'd housed inside his cave.

"You are right," she called, her voice drowning out the

true trajectory of her thoughts. "I would be foolish to throw in my lot with these two when I might join your side instead."

Lefre chuckled, straightening slightly as he shifted away from Emryc. His blade still rested on the warrior's neck.

"Allow me, fair king, the offering of a story, one dear to my people in such times as these."

The king's gaze narrowed slightly.

"Ignore his posturing, my Chosen." Cassandra's lulling voice drowned out the torrent of her thoughts. *"Your path is right. Go on."*

The evergreen blaze of Emryc's eyes protested. Daugath's blue-white fear . . . she could see it now. Desperation drove him. He had seized the one chance he believed he would find.

Circe stilled the sounds of her deep-set thoughts and allowed her voice to rise above their rushing waters. "The tale is an offering to you, my king. A sign of loyalty." She conjured false memories of bowing before other sovereigns, weaving tales of splendor for the delight of their surface-dwelling courts.

Lefre nodded once. "Very well. Let us see this magic my ex-general spoke so highly of."

The saudad smiled and dipped into a bow as best she could around the fomorian guard's grasp. His arm loosened slightly, just as she had hoped. "As you wish, my lord."

Circe willed an added brightness to her eyes and enhanced the shimmer of her skin. Around the chamber, the lanterns stilled their drifting. "An ancient magic ties my people to the woven fate of the world," she began, "the threads deeper embedded than those that hold any other."

Her mother had been the first to tell her of Cassandra's

binding spells over their people, a sign of the goddess's mercy after their home city of Orison fell. "Travelers by nature, we could not return home after our beloved city vanished from the face of Eldura."

With each retelling, the story embedded itself deeper into her bones. Cassandra had chosen her people, yes, but they had each chosen her as well. *We carry her stories.*

The guard's hold loosened further. Her tale's ropes were beginning to take hold.

"This special fate started with a single storyteller, trapped alone in the dark, whom the goddess rescued. 'If you accept my help,' the goddess said, 'you and your people will become bearers of my magic through the ages. The stories of fate will bind themselves to you and you to them.' The power and promise of what she offered glimmered in Cassandra's eyes. 'Their deep-set magic shall be yours alone to wield.'"

A half-smile tugged at the corner of Lefre's mouth. He pictured himself in possession of this power, exactly as she had wished.

"The goddess told the lost saudad the parameters of her binding. 'I cannot restore what you have lost, but I can weave your destiny anew.' The lost saudad assented, joining our destiny to fate's very thread. She swore herself and her people to serve the goddess.

"Tears gathered in Cassandra's eyes. This binding was not without cost. 'If you accept this, you will never return home.'" Circe's voice grew thick.

"The lost saudad shook her head. 'We will forge a new home, woven from your stories.' At this, the goddess smiled. The saudad would soon know the weight of their binding, for fortune's wheel ever turns." Circe steadied her breath, clutching the ropes of her story-bindings. Soon, she would unleash the magic she had coiled. "Through ages we wander, our home in our hearts. We, and we alone, know the sorrow and power of what Cassandra's binding wrought."

Emerald light crackled in Circe's gaze as she turned her eyes upon the king. Her voice grew loud, resounding across the hall. "This power I now call." Circe threw her shoulder back into the guard who held her. He grunted as he stumbled back, granting her the sliver of freedom she needed.

"By darkness and vine," she chanted, "by depths be undone." Waves of energy lapped up from her depths, rising swiftly through the chasm she'd crafted.

The king grimaced, his fire-hued face flaring scarlet. "Stop her," he ordered his guards.

In unison, the fomorian soldiers surrounded her.

She slid away from the one holding her to the center of the circle.

Metal screeched as they withdrew their curved blades.

"Circe!" Emryc shouted. The warrior flung himself from the axe blade, offsetting the king's stance. Blood sprayed in his wake. In a fluid motion, he thrust himself over the line of lanterns, his wings unfurled.

Blinding rays exploded out of the lanterns, streaking toward Emryc. They embedded themselves as radiant fire into his wings.

Circe screamed. She dodged the first guard who lunged at her and took aim through the gap in the circle he left.

Emryc cried out as he plummeted toward the ground. His brilliant black feathers that shone emerald in the sun withered, sizzling as he shouted in pain.

The saudad thrust her hands forward, the fury of fate

at her fingertips as she aimed for the lanterns. She would break through their protective barrier around the king.

"Good." Daugath's voice murmured into the roar of her mind. *"You remembered."* The ghost of his bright smile flared across her vision.

Daugath tugged the gem free from his chest. He slammed its tip into the temple of the guard nearest him. The fomorian soldier crumpled immediately beneath the blow, the garnet light of his gemstone extinguished.

"Kill them all!" the king bellowed.

The circle of soldiers around Circe closed tight. A cruel laugh broke free from one soldier's lips.

Beyond the deadly ring of their blades, Emryc struggled to rise.

He fought for her still. Circe blinked back the tears that rose. If only she could speak directly into his mind. *For you I weave my final tale.* Ancient magic thrummed deep within. She knew not what unleashing it would mean.

Another blade swung for her waist. She spun away in time. Her movement sent her crashing into one of the bare-chested soldiers behind. His ruby stone grazed the top of her shoulder. Her skin heated as blood pooled.

But the lunges of blade-wielding soldiers provided her the angle she needed.

Circe narrowed her gaze to the king.

"By darkness and vine," she growled this time, "by depths be undone." Circe flung her arm from hip to shoulder, directing the line of ancient magic she'd conjured where it should strike the king.

The air beside her trembled. A cold tongue of iron sang closer.

Sparks of black flame glowed from her fingertips.

Across the room, ebony ropes wrapped around the torso of the king, binding him from hip to shoulder.

Circe screamed as one of the guard's blades tore into her outstretched arm. Pain as she had never known it hurtled through her veins.

King Lefre's eyes widened. He released a single gasp.

The vines cinched tight, slicing his body in half. They vanished into nothing. With a sickening thump, the king's head and severed shoulder struck the ground.

Circe's forearm—cut free by the guard's blade—thunked onto the stone beside her. The black vines slithered toward her from behind her eyes, obscuring her vision. *The story's magic, it had claimed her soul as well.*

Instead of chaos, a pale purple light pierced the room.

Daugath's voice echoed from the rafters. "You are bound now to me, my brethren. The dark of the old has turned over. A new time arrives with me as your king . . ."

Strong arms caught her around the waist and held her close. "Hold on, Circe." *A voice she knew.* "Don't leave me here." *Emryc.* His fingers brushed the side of her face. A blurred teardrop fell from his dark eyelashes onto her cheek. "I promised that I would return you to the light."

CHAPTER 23

"THE HOLE IN THE VINES"

As Cassandra taught us, there once was a girl with vines for arms who lived in the ivy-covered hole of her heart. When she first arrived, there weren't many vines. The space between the sides of the hole seemed impossibly far. But little by little, the girl grew her vines, reaching and wending their way across the expanse between the two sides.

It was not soon, but one day, as the vines continued to grow, the girl found they were thick enough for her to walk from one side to the other. She wasn't sure what she would find on the other side of the hole.

But the girl was brave and curious, driven by a desire to explore.

She wrapped her vine arms around the ropes of ivy nearest her. Fear gripped her throat. *What would happen if she fell deeper into the pit?* She had tried not to think about that first day when she arrived, the long fall she'd had before she landed here.

The girl shook her doubts free. There was time to think on this later. She extended the vines of her arms once again. With enough patience and practice—she steadied herself—she could walk across the thread from one side to the next.

Her first journey was frightening. The chasm below stretched deep. Sound only came from herself and the song of her vines. "Help me to cross," she whispered out into the darkness. "I need to see the other side."

Subsequent journeys grew easier, and the girl learned to feel more at home in the dark. From her first path she made others, and soon a complex web of vines spanned the distances that stretched over the black expanse.

But no matter how thoroughly she wove her ivy strands, a hole in the middle remained. She tried many techniques, thin braided lines and overgrown branches. Still, they shriveled away. They left only black space behind. "Why will this not work?" the girl said to herself and her vines. Was she not meant to span the hole into which she had fallen?

She stomped across her winding vine path to the side of the hole and peered in.

The girl leapt back as a pair of eyes blinked up at her out of the dark.

"Gods!" the girl cried. "Who are you?"

Her heart caught in her throat as the figure emerged. Iridescent emerald wings fluttered free.

An onyx-clad faery with midnight-blue skin and eyes gray as the sea turned to stare at the girl, a serene smile upon her face. "One day, when you're ready, you will see."

Time continued to pass in the hole in the dark, buried deep inside the lost girl's heart.

Her new faery friend wove stories to cheer the girl. For

the first time, flowers blossomed along the vines that spanned the darkness.

"I still don't understand," the girl said with a frown, gazing again into the dark of the faery's domain. "Why can my vines not cross this spot? It makes even the flowers wither away."

"Are you sure you are ready?" The faery raised a dark eyebrow.

"Please, I think it is time." The girl settled at the edge of the hole. She wrapped one ankle over the other and clutched her knees tight to her chest.

"As you wish." The faery nodded. "I am memories of what you have lost," the faery explained.

Around them, the plant-song rose. The flowers danced on their stems.

"Your vines cannot bridge me, for to my gaps they lead." The memory faery smiled and shook her head. "I will remain here as long as you will, until you're ready to return once more to the light. But this hole, it will linger after us, where what you yearn for used to be."

The faery reached out, her hand petal-soft upon the girl's face. "What you have lost is not gone," the faery added with a tinge of concern crinkling her sea-gray eyes. "They've just changed their form."

Dark memories returned to the girl then. Flashes of lightning ravaged the expanse of woven vines. *Her white city under siege. Orison, her home, vanished beneath the roar of waves.* The girl pitched forward, falling into the darkness before her. *She could never go home again.*

Out of the darkness, the faery lunged for the girl. She propelled them both back to the spread of vines above. The hidden realization burned in the girl's eyes. Her faery held her closer still. "Let's you and I together find a new home." With the girl clasped tight, her trilling wings carried them both upward through the chasm.

The girl hugged the faery back. Vinesong rose as they flew. High above, a faint shimmer. There, a beckoning sliver of light glowed and grew.

EPILOGUE

Over the centuries of his imprisonment, Emryc had learned much of what it meant to be swept into the path of the goddess Cassandra. Tales of other Chosen trickled through Apollo's dungeons and confirmed what he had seen while he served at Circe's side.

Cassandra often gifted her representatives with prophetic visions, tellings of what is, was, and could yet be. Each Chosen had to chart their own course through these tales, slowly coming to understand the narrative behind their Sight. They would need to discern which of the visions was for them to interpret and which was merely for them to See.

Despite this gift, the goddess of fate kept her own counsel. She alone could tell why some, by their innate nature, changed the weave of fate, while others simply followed the course of their own thread.

Circe had begged Emryc to let her go, to allow her freedom. Had she known, by her request, that she condemned both him and his line to an eternity of misfortune? He had confessed his promise to Apollo shortly after they emerged from the Underland, once Circe's fever from her half-severed arm had finally abated. He hadn't known then that the wound's pain would never fully leave her. When he finally revealed the other oath he had made, she had raged against the guardian's directive. Emryc would never forget the way her emerald eyes burned as she internalized his betrayal. Her pledge, she swore, was to serve Cassandra and no other. And so he let her go.

He had sensed his curse before he met Circe—its presence had driven him to forge a bargain with Apollo—and he had grown more aware of his blighted fate while fighting to help and protect Cassandra's Chosen. But it was not until Circe's death that he looked misfortune in the eye. And in a single moment, misfortune condemned him to remain, in perpetuity, by her side. Her sour smile spread its shadow across the entirety of his line.

How often, locked away in the depths of Apollo's domain, had he questioned the goddess? *Did I not serve you loyally? Did I not protect your Chosen until she asked that I do so no more?*

But no matter the urgency of his beseeching, Cassandra remained silent.

Emryc had nearly given up hope until the worlds began to stir two decades before. Souls returned, their births foretold. Hope exhaled her spring breeze across the lands. His line, once expansive, had fallen to a single figure, a fae who wandered the Old Bastion Highlands, at times in search of a new future, at others, daring death.

The hope of victory against Alessandra was not Emryc's to partake in. And yet, when word reached him of a young saudad, born beneath the sign of the Enchantress, he could not squelch the four-petaled iris blossoming within. This, he knew, was the final chance to end his curse, to free his spirit to Astralei—where he hoped Circe waited for him still.

He could not fathom why Cassandra would appoint Jez, his heir, to watch over one of her select. His heir carried the specter of misfortune, the dark side of Cassandra's gaze—like all of his descendants after his broken vow to Apollo. Why allow Jez to doom the fate of this young saudad, in the earliest years of her adventures?

Circe had believed that Cassandra favored storytellers. "Take the thread of fate into your own hands," she would have told him. "Weave a new narrative for yourself, one without me." She had believed in different types of Chosen, ones who selected themselves as well as those appointed by a deity. It was easy to see why Circe, blessed by fate herself, had seen the world in this way.

But each life Emryc had touched ended in death and misfortune.

Apollo was right to punish him, to rend his wings from his back and lock him away, alone in a world of memories. Inside his cage, he endangered no one.

"One day, you and your descendants will break the curse," Circe had told him. "When you find the Lady of Fortune, she will show you the way."

The dungeon door banged open, startling Emryc from his account to Cerdris, his casting of the world of memory.

Apollo's cold voice echoed down. "It is time for you and your line to prove your worth to me," he ordered. "Come, and speak to me of this heir of yours."

Emryc stifled a groan as he pushed himself to standing and stepped free from the candlelight of Cerdris's small desk in the dungeon. Still trapped inside the cage, his wings whispered. Emryc refused to give Apollo the satisfaction of gazing back at them through the darkness. That part of his story was done.

"We'll continue this later," he said to Cerdris, dismissing the story-stealer.

"What am I to do now?" the writer called after him.

Emryc shook his head, neglecting to answer. *Do as you see fit.* He stalked up the shadow-stairway that wound through the depths of the guardian's domain. "Have you arranged for them to meet?" Emryc glared up at his captor. Apollo had swelled his size so that he might glower down at the one who had failed him in the ages before.

Apollo smiled, and a burst of cold thrashed through Emryc's veins. "Yes," he said. "Their paths will cross at Caisteal Tulach."

Emryc blanched. The guardian couldn't be serious. After the siege, their enemy knew—

"Much has changed in your absence." Apollo crossed his arms, his eyes slits of gold boring into Emryc's own. "With my help, the castle is once again a fortification of which we can be proud, its shelter secure."

Emryc shifted on the stair, testing the free movement of his limbs.

"You have Juliet to thank for this opportunity," Apollo continued. "She thought you and your line deserved the best chance to lend your support." The guardian inclined his head, indicating that Emryc should follow. "We shall see if the vulpine can convince Persephonie of the same."

Emryc bit back his retort. He had been right to allow Circe the freedom of death she had sought. *Seizing the thread of fate indeed.* He could only hope, for Persephonie's sake, that she was both more pliable and more smiled upon by fortune than even Circe had been. *She will need it, to withstand such times, and to perceive the dangers waiting without and within.*

⊛

CASSANDRA LEANED BACK AGAINST HER AMETHYST throne, a wide smile stretching across her lips. The image of Emryc trudging up the endless stairs after Apollo faded. Emryc had indeed increased in wisdom over the years of his imprisonment, as she had promised Circe he might. He had learned more secure soil in which to plant his hope, though he could not yet perceive his own role in the tapestry of destiny. Because of his sacrifice, the surrender of his love and devotion, Persephonie had inherited a wealth of stories Circe had not had access to, including those of the first Chosen.

The true question, she mused, and perhaps one only the goddess of fate could see, was not whether Emryc's heir could faithfully guide Persephonie.

No. Could Jez first learn the importance of choosing oneself, of wrapping one's hands around the binding weave of fate, seizing the path as one's own? Could Jez learn to trust Persephonie and not the curse Emryc and his lineage knew so well? Then, and only then, could his heir help Persephonie become the Chosen she was meant to be.

Cassandra twirled her fingers through curling locks of onyx hair. "We shall see," the goddess whispered to herself. "We shall see."

Dorric Themear has experienced the giddy flutterings of new love before. But not like this. Behind the sapphire eyes of Lady Emelyee Amastacia lies a long-awaited destiny that neither of them can sense or stop.

However, forces darker than Emelyee's husband are prepared to stand in their way.

Ridel, one of Lucien's most trusted servants, is less than enthused about her assignment to watch the lovers. If only her master had been visionary enough to see that a child cannot result if the parents are dead. She'll do her best to comply with his orders to watch and to wait—at least for now.

High in the Frostmaw Mountains, Yvayne has seen the signs of a turning of the age before. Perhaps this time, with the proper intervention, she and the druids can make a play for Azuria after all.

Visit bethballbooks.com/join to join our reading community, and you'll receive a free copy of *Aurora*, the prequel novella for the *Age of Azuria* series. Find out where Iellieth's story truly began!

Beth Ball is an epic fantasy author telling stories in the world of Azuria. When she's not writing fantasy fiction, Beth is a tabletop RPG designer and a literary scholar. Her academic work focuses on contemporary novels that encourage readers to find agency and empowerment in their approach to nature and their impact on the natural world, and her TTRPG adventures incorporate lots of druids.

You can find her and more stories set in Azuria at bethballbooks.com.

twitter.com/GroveGuardian

instagram.com/bethballauthor

Thank you for reading *Story Magic*! If you enjoyed this novella, please take a moment to leave a review. That helps so much, and I appreciate your time in doing so!

I'm sure you noticed connections to *Hadvarian Heist* across this novella, but I wanted to point out a few that were especially fun for me to work with. First, Persephonie calls upon the magic described in "The Legend of Enidia" in her battle against Aylin in Tempus Market. And second, "Legend of the Black Oak Forest" ties to the dryad Iellieth meets before venturing to Nocturne. We may even find elements of this story returning in *Amber Queen* . . .

ACKNOWLEDGMENTS

First and foremost, my gratitude to my amazing editor, Kristen. Your encouragement around what this novella *could* be fertilized the seed of the novella is was and allowed it to grow into the interconnected web of stories that it is. Thank you.

To Anjanee, my cover designer: The picture of Persephonie on the front of this novella is so completely perfect and provided a beam of inspiration during the cloudy moments of creation.

To Jonathan, who explores this amazing world with me each week—none of these stories would exist without you.

To Kelly, thank you for your careful hand and precision.

And finally, to you, dear reader: I hope you enjoyed the stories within these pages as much as I have loved sharing them with you. Thank you to those of you who have reached out to share your favorite moments and characters from *Age of Azuria*. That means more than I can say!

www.ingramcontent.com/pod-product-compliance
Lightning Source LLC
Chambersburg PA
CBHW021151190726
48288CB00008B/2929